# A BAD PIECE OF LUCK

## By Tom Abrams

## LIVINGSTON UNIVERSITY PRESS

ISBN 0-942979-22-3 cloth
ISBN 0-942979-23-0 paper

Library of Congress Catalog Number: 94-78598


First edition

Livingston University Press
Station 22
Livingston, AL 35470


Cover photos (front and back): Skip Harris
Typesetting and layout: Joe Taylor and Gerald Jones


We wish to thank the following people for their help in proof-reading and for their comments: Jane Duke, Chris Dyer, Charles Loveless, Holly McKinney, Tina Naremore, Mary Pagliero, and Victoria Purvis.

Printed in the United States of America.

Printing by Birmingham Publishing Company

# A BAD PIECE OF LUCK

*This book is for Robert Smith and Keli Baer,*
*who have moved away.*

# 1. TAMPA AUTUMN (1982)

"How come they so yella colored like that?"

"They butter cats," O'Neil said.

O'Neil had reddish-blond hair with a short, bad haircut, a big handlebar mustache and three-day beard. His face was sunburned. It was lined so he looked older than he was and held an expression always that was a little sleepy. He was thin to the point his body seemed almost disconnected in places. He sat at the old card table under the live oak, honing his jackknife. There were seven catfish on a stringer in the grass.

He regarded Kuka a moment, then got to smiling to where it made spurs along his eyes and spoke as follows:

"You lookin' rough, boy. You jus' kind a hauntish lookin' this mornin'. There ain't no else way to put it."

"I got too much sleep," Kuka said. It had been the first night he'd slept good in nearly a week.

"You might need to sort your ass out some now."

Somewhat later, when nothing else had been said, Kuka scowled at the sun.

"The hell time is it?" he said.

"It ain't but nine," O'Neil said, "but I swear, this heat's 'bout to addle my brain a'ready."

He walked to the bed of his old Dodge pickup, got a hammer, a can of nails, pliers and a bucket. A mockingbird started to sing, jumping up and down insanely on the telephone wire. Across the street kudzu entwined the abandoned gas station and its fading R.C. Cola sign.

"Somethin's riled that bird. It's begun to put me in mind a that preacher we had oncet when we was children. Sometimes he'd get to such a heavenly pitch, he'd talk in a language no one could understand but the Lord."

"I think it's jus' gone mad," Kuka said.

"There you go," O'Neil said. He nailed the catfish to the oak, a 16-penny nail through each of their heads, made a cross on their backs with the knife blade, then took the pliers and skinned them. Afterwards, he cut the bodies from the heads and threw the meat into the bucket.

"Them cooters gone dormant, or jus' they wadn't hungry," he said. "Weren't nary a one. But I still got a icebox full. You'll have to come over for supper a night."

Kuka only nodded.

The last time he'd eaten there, O'Neil's wife, Leona, had made turnip greens and blue jay. After which O'Neil'd commented, "Mother, that was some fine eatin'.""

"I got a fix on that rooster," O'Neil said. "It's them niggers what got it. Them over there catty-corner behind that little grocery store. Why anybody'd keep a rooster in the city for is beyond me."

Kuka said, "First chance I get, I'm gone wind that sonbitch up."

"I mean," O'Neil said.

O'Neil was relating then how he'd caught the cats in the old phosphate pit he frequented, "At the edge of the bonnets, directly out from that black persimmon ..." when Kuka noticed him look to the side of the house. Kuka turned then, and it was Wade. Wade Bonner stood there, blunt, stocky, that movie star Irish face, his eyes penetrating but at the same time preoccupied and telling nothing.

"Hey," Kuka said. "Where you been?"

"I forget her name," Wade said.

Wade looked past Kuka then and said, "Hey, O'Neil."

O'Neil paid his regards, but he understood that something was up. He'd done a three-year stretch in Raiford for manslaughter a time back, and though he was through with all that, it had left him cautious. So he now politely left the conversation.

"We gone shut down," Wade said. "Cecil touted on me to the police."

After a moment, Kuka said, "I knew Cecil was trouble."

"Yeah, well ... that ain't what matters. The thing is, the cops got my name. So get the shit out the house. Take it over to Roy L.'s. He's back. I jus' talked to him. An' take out a pound a smoke for Deuce. He can get a good price at the tables. So's we'll have some cash till this thing cools down. An' get my pistol." He started to leave.

"Where you goin'?"

"I'm lookin' for Cecil's ass. Gone. I got a cab waitin'. An' you hear anything, leave a message at the bar."

Kuka walked over to the water spigot, where O'Neil was filleting the catfish.

"I wish he wouldn't be orderin' me around like that," he said.

"He wadn't orderin' you."

"What'd you call it then?"

"Well," O'Neil said. He lit a cigarette and thought for a moment. O'Neil liked to measure his words to make sure they fit. "He does have a bad case a sayin' what he means. Sort a cuts through the smoke right to the meat. But I believe he 'as jus' tryin' to kick-start you, now. Look Kuka," he said, "you still sleep with your hat on?"

"Yeah. So what?" Kuka pulled his ballcap down tighter on his head.

"You knock on the icebox 'fore you open it, like you used to?"

"Yeah. So what's yer point?"

But Kuka wasn't paying so much attention to the conversation. *Cecil*, he was thinking. Cecil was a pimp, and he always had three, four people looking for him. "Don't call me Cecil no more," he'd say. "I'm the Greek." Kuka had heard him introduce himself that way. But everyone who knew him called him Cecil anyway, and it drove him nuts. On top of this, he was a harelip. Whether or not this had anything to do with him being an asshole, no one ever thought too much about it. But he was one of them people Kuka couldn't ever figure why Bonner hung around with—other than to keep himself sharp. Because Cecil always had some kind of snag going.

O'Neil said, "I seen a deer this mornin'. Lord it was pretty out there. Like as if the whole mornin' was a animal bein' still, an' the wild things was snorin'. I come 'round that cypress head below the pit. It was a little doe, no farther'n you away ... an' her ears was just a blinkin' at me."

Kuka looked at him like he was a distant point on the map.

"Wha'd you say O'Neil? I heard ya an' I didn't."

"It wadn't nothin'."

"O'Neil ... you know Cecil?"

"I don't know that crowd. Don't want a. Look," O'Neil said. He pointed to the catfish heads nailed to the tree. They were all still trying to breathe.

Well after awhile, O'Neil asked Kuka if he cared to burn one, so they smoked some of O'Neil's very own, a purple-stripe variety that he grew and, far as Kuka understood, had invented. You couldn't take very much of it. It would leave you bewildered for an hour or so.

Some time later, a couple neighborhood kids, on the front sidewalk busting caps with a hammer, brought him out of it. Kuka noticed that he was sitting at the card table alone, and he speculated that O'Neil had left.

He checked his blue jeans. He hadn't even enough change for breakfast. He observed too that his jeans pretty much stank. A sadness would overtake him at these moments.

He looked over to the clothesline, to a pair of his shorts that had been hanging there about a week. He went to take the shorts off the line, but as he did so, he discovered a little Carolina wren in one of the pockets. The wren flew off, and Kuka watched it in wonder.

There were two leaves and a long piece of string in that pocket.

And that was the start of it. It'd take him some three months to realize this, but it was the little wren that began it all. For what the wren had left in his pocket that day turned out to be the unexpected side of things.

## 2. RED ASS

*The pistol.* It was something Kuka didn't catch up to for a time. Then he remembered that it was cached in Madonna's fireplace. From this he understood right off, as he said to his mind, It's one them things, where the more you stir it, the more it's gone stink. Because Wade had on the same clothes he'd had on the last time Kuka'd seen him, it meant probably that he'd gone off with some angel for a couple, three days and left all his gear at Madonna's. He'd been pretty much staying over there at her house for awhile.

What filled him with such sadness at this point was the fact that Madonna Smith had the worst temper he'd ever witnessed in a beautiful woman. Don't get it wrong. Kuka'd known his share of mean women. But they was always kind of ugly, or broad of beam, or plain in the mind. Madonna wasn't none of these. What she did have was a bold mouth. At the very least, Kuka reckoned, he would be asked to turn over the name of that what Wade had been staying with. That Wade Bonner had foreseen all this wasn't never in question. So Kuka just stood there a minute and cussed him.

He took the alley to Roy L.'s. The alley was all potholes. Every manner of dog in the backyards barked at him behind their fences, but you would never see anybody there except kids who weren't up to no good to start with.

In Kuka's frame was laziness and strength, fat and muscle. His hair, which he spent little time on, was totally irreconcilable and stuck out at every angle under his ballcap. At one moment he would seem to be gazing inwardly—it was an expression both curious and singular to him—as if he'd forgotten something that would let it all make sense. At the next, his dark eyes looked hard about him. He was carrying jail time in the rucksack.

He sweat from the heat. It was that part of October in Tampa where the entire town waits for the first day of fall. In the streets, the neighborhood bars, cigar factories, down at the Air Force base, the breweries, phosphate mines, the docks and brothels, people turned to one another and said, "It's been hot too long." The light had turned flat, but there was an indolence about, and the temperature would not break. By afternoon, the day would get so hot it'd make you angry to be out in it.

Now, if you walked up Central Avenue in Seminole Heights that morning and looked to your left just past Jimmy's Barber Shop, you might have seen Kuka and Roy L. in the shade of a pecan tree looking for nuts.

Roy L. was from Ville Platte, Louisiana. Actually, he'd tell you, a little place outside that called Millers Lake. He was a plumber by trade. At the bar he'd picked up the handle of Spotter, for his knack of seeing things first. If you was trying to avoid some girl, say, or catch up with a bet you'd made, when they come in, he'd be the first to point it out. Otherwise, he never did talk so much. He was kind of shy. He was someone foreign in his slang. And talking with him one on one, it was more like he'd agree pretty much with what you just said.

"Poo-yie! I see what you been say...." He had on green work clothes, the pant cuffs tucked inside his boots.

Some three weeks earlier, he'd gone up to visit friends on the St. Johns River, and he'd just stayed on. Come back with stories of shine being cooked in the hammocks, of taking 'shrooms and having a big red dog follow him around for days afterwards, a dog that only he could see, and of a girl he'd met who was hard to let go of, the dream and despair of the young men of Palatka. In the meantime, he'd lost his job. And his uncle, who was his only kin in town, thought that he'd come in harm's way.

"Yer Uncle Joe come around," Kuka said. "You'd been gone maybe a week, ten days. He come by. He's kind of a natural worrier ain't he? He thought you was killed, or in jail. But I'm goin' to myself, *Shit ... he's jus' holed up with an angel*. But I didn't say nothin'. I jus' told him, 'I don't know. I couldn't tell you, Joe.'

"There ain't much goin' on at the bar. Wade's got it calm. The men don't fight there no more. Now it's jus' the women wantin' to kick ass on one another."

Roy L. got to laughing at that.

"Mickey's been had some things of note. He ain't gone give you no deal though, you know. But it's jus' nice to buy one a them sawbucks a his. Puts you right. An' he don't step on it so bad as he used to.

"But far as it stayin' calm, you watch. Wade'll fix that. It's one them home-made laws a his. Things too quiet, you jus' fucking put an end to that. Otherwise, pretty soon, ole Shorty Powers, he'll start thinkin' he don't need a bouncer there no more.

"Did I tell you Mickey got fired again?"

"What he done now?" Roy L. said.

"He kept sucker-punchin' everybody. He's barred this time. Can't even go in there to buy a drink. But he still hangs out in the parkin' lot.... Look sideways at his girl, he'd nail 'em. I seen him do it. This dude, he was lightin' a cigarette at the time. Mick caught him flush from the side. But it ain't the punch hurt him so as when his head hit the floor.

"I swear," Kuka added, "that girl a Mick's, she jus' ain't no good. Yeah, I know, Mickey, he ain't no prize his self. He's a junkie, there ain't much else to say on it. But you can't help likin' him.

"An' he shaved his head. Lord, all them old scars. Makes you sad to think on it. But one night some time back ... maybe I told you this 'fore you left, when he sucker-punched that big ole boy? Then he bit his ear off? Well you know how Mick's got that front tooth missin' ... so this boy come back last week. Him an' his brother, who talked sort a funny. This little asshole with a gun what ain't concealed too good. They come in the bar. An' you could see how that big boy's ear'd healed up. But there's this little tab stickin' out where that missin' tooth don't catch nothin'.

"Or say, you remember that old preacher comes in? Got a pretty young wife? Parson Honeywood they call him. I don't know what he is, some kind a holy-roller. He didn't go to school. Jus' one day he said, 'I'm a preacher.' He got the callin'. He's the guy that testifies out in the parkin' lot sometimes.

"Well him and his wife come in the other night, an' you know how it is there, how it's all up for grabs ... you see a man with that you might want a dance with, go stand behind it, see how true she is? So this cowboy's hangin' around, an' the preacher's wife gives him the lazy eye. She's always beggin' on the side anyways, an' they go dance a slow one...."

Kuka paused here to swallow a pecan he'd been chewing on.

"So what the preacher said?" Roy L. asked.

"He don't say nothin'! He takes out a knife ... an' damn if he don't stab himself in the leg. I mean! That'll teach the bitch.

"You got yer deck? Let's go play some Red Ass.... I don't know, Roy L.—I jus' don't know what street some a these sports live on."

# 3. A PAIR TO DRAW TO

While they were under the pecan tree, which was to the front of
Roy L.'s place, Emmett Pike came jogging up. Emmett was not the
picture of health as might be imagined here. He had that barroom
pallor, and his legs were skinny and white, as though he'd kept them
forever in a closet. For most the time he would only go out after it was
dark. He'd taken up running, but he had not culled his other habits in
the least. He'd cached a bottle of Tanqueray at Roy L.'s and several
other places along his route.

Emmett's true name was well known, but he was called Deuce by
most everyone. He always wore glasses so dark, say like at that moment, Kuka and Roy L. must have appeared as the Jack of Clubs, Jack
of Spades. They went inside and made arrangements for the pound.

"Kuka," Deuce said. He'd made himself a gin and tonic and was
just lighting a cigarette. "You recall them too little gals you seen the
other day ... out back a my place?"

There were two sisters lived next door to Deuce up by the inter-
state. One of them was 14 and the other younger. They had hair that
was long and yellow as lemons, with freckles all over their faces. Their
skin was very light, and they had blue eyes that was different than any
kind he had ever seen before. But though they were young, they'd
grown up in Sulphur Springs and knew the score. They were young
and curious about things, but they were not exactly fire bright.

Kuka had walked out back one day at Deuce's. Deuce had just
given them each a quarter. The older one popped the quarter in her
mouth and started chewing it. Then he went inside, and the girls
started talking to Kuka. They were big talkers, especially the younger
one—mostly about the good-looking boys in the neighborhood. The
little one began telling him about this punk that lived upstairs.

"He kissed us," she said. "On the lips."

"When do I get mine?" Kuka asked.

The young one made a face. She claimed to be 13, but her older
sister laughed when this was said.

"You got gray in your beard. An' you ain't handsome neither.
You jus' look kind a...." He believed "peculiar" was what she was
after, but she couldn't find it, and Kuka said:

"Gray, my ass."

The older one, she didn't say nothing. She just chewed her quarter.

"Yeah," Kuka said to Deuce now. "I remember."

"Well see," Deuce said, "the older one ... she took the loggerhead,
buddy. I couldn't even get it in all the way." He shook his head and

smiled like a dog. "Now her sister's jealous. Can you beat it? I mean, hell, they're young ... but you can't hold that against 'em."

He finished his gin and tonic, put out a cigarette, left the apartment and started jogging awkwardly, against the grain, the road sliding away from him somehow.

"It's the heat," Kuka observed. "It don't break soon, we all gonna be in deep shit."

Kuka cracked a pecan, ate half of it (it was much too green), then got a look on his face—a strange mixture of wonder and serenity. For right at that moment he felt a kind of blind confidence in the belief that one day soon the tide must turn. Why he felt this will never be known. "It's hotter'n a jalapeño," he added.

Roy L. only nodded. Like has been said, he wasn't one to ramble on. For this reason it was a pleasure for Kuka to talk with him. Most everyone else he knew, they couldn't say enough. They'd bend his ear. You gotta have someone to talk with, Kuka said to his mind. Someone to listen, who don't have no grudge in the way, or a girl between you, or something to prove.

Kuka'd brought along some of O'Neil's catfish, and Roy L. started frying them up. As he did this, amid the sporadic popping of the grease, he spoke about this girl he was sweet on:

"She jus' made 18 year old," he said. "But she know where ever' t'ang at. Know how it woik. She got a boyfrien', see ... he trouble, him. His name Skunk."

"Skunk?" Kuka asked.

"At's what I said. What kind a name ...

"I took her out jukin'. We had mos' bes' time ... I tell you what. But she go be wid him, den come to me. Some nights maybe she fuckin' ever'body, I don' know. After 'while, I tole her, I can't do it. I don't can no more. I'm goin' 'way, now—get out cheer. For her to made up her mind. But chu know ... I can't help but feel 'bout her. She call, man, I goin' bag dere.

"Her boyfrien' ... I say, Fuck it. So I put da *gris-gris* on 'im." He made his hands move like a spider will do when it's tightening its web. "Where y'at, Skunk? He ain't even know 't chet, but he gone. *Gris-gris* gone fuck 'im over." Then he laughed like hell.

Now Kuka understood from previous conversations with him that the *gris-gris* was some kind of swamp hex. Roy L. had odd notions such as this. But he laughed like hell, and Kuka thought, Damn ... this boy is come undone a little bit over her.

Well Kuka had finished eating and was wiping his hands on his shorts when Mickey drove up in his old red Studebaker. It was probably the last Studebaker in town, and why it still ran no one was sure. "You gettin' a bit of everything through here this mornin'," Kuka said.

Mickey got out of the car and sidled up to the kitchen window. He'd broken his right leg in a motorcycle accident many years back on a Alabama highway road. It was a bad wreck, and he just kind of dragged that leg.

Now Mickey always looked at you, even after he'd known you for a long time, like he was sizing you up. He stayed outside and spoke through the screen.

"Smells like fish," he said. "You eatin' fish for breakfast?"

Roy L. said, "You want? We got dat or pecan or boat."

Mickey's eyes got a flat look to them.

"Kuka ... he's talkin' like that again," he said.

Roy L. turned to Kuka and said, "What it is, a joke?"

"I don't eat breakfast," Mickey said. "I got beer." He looked at the bottle in his hand. There seemed to be a still moment in time.

"You up early," Kuka said.

"I ain't been to bed yet," he said. "Kuka, look ... you got any cash money?"

Now if you saw Mickey for two minutes, he'd ask you for three things. So it was good to start off saying no to this and no to that.

Kuka said, "I'm tapped out."

"Where the hell was you last night?"

"I went to the dog track," Kuka said. He'd taken thirty bucks with him, but he got there early and spent a good part of this on hot dogs and beer before the races started. Then he'd made several wild bets.

"Let me hold a fin," Mickey said. "I know yer flush."

"I got shit. Come on. Who you talkin' to...."

"You got anything to roll while we discuss this?"

"Talk to Deuce. He's got some."

"He has a knot in his pocket," Mickey said. "Say ... is he been by here yet?"

"You jus' missed him."

"Oh, that's too bad. I was hopin' we could towel each other off." Mick didn't think too much of exercise, see.

"Talk to Cecil," Kuka said. "He likes to talk."

"He's in jail," Mickey said.

Well the day was sort of taken back there awhile, got drawn into the cobwebs and dust and holes in the window screen, and everything leaned like Mickey toward his busted leg.

"You got a cigarette?"

"Yeah," Kuka said. "Mick ... I need a favor. Drive me down to Madonna's. I gotta pick up Wade's gear. He ain't stayin' there no more."

Mickey seemed to study the window frame awhile.

"So what yer talkin' 'bout," he said finally, "is breakin' in?"

"That'd be preferable," Kuka said.

"Them two's on the outs?" Mickey asked.

"I guess."

Mickey dwelled on that some.

"I wouldn't mind pickin' up some the slack on that," he said.

Mickey got a cigarette and dime and drove on to the telephone booth at the 7-Eleven to call Madonna's, make sure she wasn't around.

After he left, Kuka was thinking on the last time he'd seen Wade. It'd been three nights back. He'd only seen him for a moment. But he'd heard him pretty much all night. Wade'd brought somebody home after work. They was hitting at it good in the living room. It sounded like they were playing basketball out there.

Whoever it was, she was gone in the morning, and Wade too. As Kuka was thinking on this, Roy L. asked, "What Mick's las' name?"

"He's got two a them," Kuka answered.

Roy L. blinked a couple times at that, then went back to reading the sports pages.

"Who's pitchin' tonight in the Series?" Kuka asked.

"Andujar an' Vuckovich."

"That'll be a game, there."

Roy L. said, "Fuckin' A."

# 4. BREAK IN

Mickey dropped him off and went on to the next block over. Madonna lived down in Hyde Park in a big white house of gables and gingerbread, with lace curtains in all the windows. Her ex-husband had dealt Harley-Davidson's, made his living off The Breed, was how rumor had it. And that he disappeared in the newspapers one day some years back. There was a hopscotch square drawn in purple chalk on the sidewalk leading to the kitchen door. Kuka broke a jalousie pane, reached his hand in. She had a piano, and paintings on the walls. Or say it smelled like apples inside. There wasn't even no dishes in the sink. Wade's gear was all there in a pile by the door. She's a lady, Kuka thought. Quite a lady. She didn't throw his shit out on the lawn as had happened a time or two before.

He took the pistol from the fireplace. Then he heard voices outside. He looked down at Wade's old suitcase. At *Scottsdale.*

*There was good news and Bad News at the Civic Plaza Thursday night. The good news is that Edgar (Bad News) Barnes did his thing again. Barnes, one of the hottest items on the American boxing scene, ran his pro record to 8-0 and registered his sixth knockout, disposing of highly regarded Wade Bonner in 1:10 of the second round. Bonner didn't make it all the way through the ropes to the seats after running into a Barnes' flurry. He lay half in half out of the ring until Barnes graciously picked him up and, cradling him like a mother would her child, laid him gently upon the canvas where Referee Billy Sparks counted him out. "When I saw that vacant look on his face and noticed that he wasn't trying to move," said Barnes, "I figured I'd better try to help him." Asked what punch knocked him out, Bonner replied: "The one that hurt the most."*

He heard the voices again and looked up. He got behind a cedar chest in the bedroom, looked out to the front porch. Madonna had her back to him. She'd gotten her hair cropped since he'd seen her last, with a little rat-tail braided in the back and tied with a blue ribbon. She was talking, in the shade of the porch, to one of Cecil's sporting girls. Kuka didn't remember her name. He recognized her as a girl he'd had a short and immature conversation with at the bar once late at night, after which she'd never spoken to him again. She had spent some time as an inmate at the Women's Correctional Institute in Hardwick, Georgia, something she'd seemed quite proud of. She was thin and fraught and, as were most of Cecil's girls, a refugee from a little town somewhere in Tennessee or north Georgia.

"Who is the guy?" Madonna said.

"Jus' somebody owes Cecil a favor."

"You best consider what you're dealin' with," Madonna said.

"I'm tellin' you, this guy's a bear. He's bad as home-made hell."

"Because he's big," Madonna said, "that don't make it. You must a never seen Wade fight. He loads up big, every punch. He's got the gift of God in his hands. An' he's covered. He's got them Nam vets around him. Even Kuka, that crazy bastard, you don't know what he'd do."

The thin girl tapped her head a couple times with her finger.

"Screw him," she said. "Bonner too. I don't like the way he passes himself off. Far as I'm concerned, he ain't nothing' but a dumb mick his own self."

"That's what you know," Madonna said.

The hillbilly girl took a half-pint bottle of clear liquid from her purse. She took off the cap and offered some to Madonna.

"Smells like iodine," Madonna said. She declined it.

"Juju water," the girl said. "I'll knock one down for you." She took a hit and batted her eyes for awhile. She held the flask out in front of her then as if its presence had caught her by surprise.

She put the bottle away and said: "Cecil ... you know he's gotta play the streets ... he's always rollin' the dice. Sometimes, if I can be truthful with you, he's a horse's ass. But he ain't no snitch. That ain't somethin' you want a own."

"I can't help you," Madonna said. "Like I said, it's over between us. I don't want a talk to the fuck ... not even to set him up...."

"An' she said, you ain't nothin' but a dumb mick," Kuka repeated to Wade that night at the bar.

"I know the one yer talkin' 'bout," Wade said. "I run her out a here. Her an' some girl had a cat fight in the bathroom. They'd been snipin' at each other all night. That's one to talk. She's 'bout eat up with stupid. But say, you got the pistol?"

Kuka nodded.

"An' my gear?"

"I had to leave it. Madonna was comin' in the door. You ought a leave it, too. I shit you not. How come you only kept them tags on the suitcase what're the places you got beat in?"

Wade didn't say nothing.

"You won in a lot a towns."

"Yeah. An' I bled in some a them good."

"An' yer blind in one eye...."

"Damn it, Kuka. Don't you ever tell nobody which one." He shook his head and smiled that kid smile of his. "You know ... that girl had a lot a paintings on her walls. I thought I'd do somethin' nice for her. So I painted a picture for her. I explained myself in it ...but she didn't like dark colors."

# 5. HARD BY NOWHERE

At the bar, if Wade wasn't busy, he and Kuka would sit and talk. They most always sat at the same table if they could, a two-seater by the jukebox. Wade would take the chair in the corner created by the jukebox and the wall. He could see the floor pretty well from there, and his back was covered. They sat there now, watching two large young ladies jitterbugging out in front of them. They were exceptional dancers, very light-footed and nimble, in spite of their bulk.

"You know them two?" Wade asked Kuka.

"I've seen them before. I don't know 'em, though."

"They sisters. I was talkin' to one 'em earlier. Said she'd lost 30 pounds since the last time I'd seen her. But I couldn't tell the difference."

Kuka had just finished telling Wade the story of the day, though maybe he changed it some to his advantage.

Wade Bonner would do the same. Kuka had heard him retell a story three, four times, smoothing it out, most often getting more sharply at its humor. Or sometimes he'd elaborate it into a new thing. Anything out of the ordinary is what they talked about, and this had not been an ordinary day.

Most of Kuka's days went like so: He would stay up all night, maybe help close the bar, then go to a bottle club. There were several bottle clubs. Deuce played pool at one called The Cocked Hat. Kuka'd watch him run some tables. Deuce was different then. A part of him wood. He didn't drink when he was shooting. He could shape a table better than anyone.

Or he'd go to another club named The Upstairs Lounge. Mickey might show up there. He would have gotten rid of his girlfriend by then, and she'd be out roaming same as he was. He'd be loaded, or else just got the jones and got it bad. Girl'd come walking by, he'd say—

"Oh, my ... now wouldn't we have a time. Kuker, you see that? Her dress looked like it was covered with telephone dimes. Lord, what has been lost here, an' what can be stolen? Look at that little girl with the red dress on. I know it's out a style, that ain't what I'm sayin'."

Or maybe a girl'd come turning her head this way and that.

"She's got two faces," Mickey'd say. "Eights and Aces ... yeah, so long darlin', an' if I don't see you again, the hell with you.

"An' this man here, you notice he don't look my way. He owes me some jack on a bet we had. Said he'd get it to me Friday when he got paid. Come to find out, he don't work."

There were girls there that was fast and loose and knew all the numbers of the songs on the jukebox. One of them might then put some music in it—a song about a 1957 Chevrolet car, and how freedom's but a prison where you're always looking for the bars.

Sometime before dawn the lights would come on. And afterward, when everything'd been said and done, they'd stand on the wild electrical street corners singing in strange voices.

It was how they put their mark on the earth then, doing hard time in Tampa, Florida, 5 a.m.

Kuka seldom remembered the details of what he did in these clubs. For a long time he stopped going to them. One night in the parking lot of The Cocked Hat he saw a kid push over a dumpster. He was mad about something. The dumpster was empty—but still in all. Then he ran away like a deer. Everyone just turned and looked at someone else to see if he had witnessed it. The person Kuka happened to look at was the girl he'd been talking to all night. She wasn't looking at him then. She was watching a biker take a piss. He was trolling. He was all but pissing on her shoe. This is nuts, Kuka thought. I don't need this.

It would be like that. He would have to be surrounded by people, and then something would happen, and he'd want to be alone all the time. Then he'd stay home. People would come around, sure. To buy reef or whatever. But he could hardly wait to get them out of the house. He just felt like being private. Girls would come around. Sometimes they'd pass each other coming and going. Maybe he would have to introduce them. The married ones fell in love desperately, but they always had to be somewhere, so, far as he was concerned, that was fine with him.

At the end of any particular night, he would not go to sleep so much as he would pass out. It was the only way he could sleep—was to drink. When Wade had the night off, on Monday or Tuesday, they'd go around to the bars and sell Quaaludes and Dilaudid. To the underworld. The junkie bars. A couple places that punkers hung out. They were very popular. The crowd would start falling off the stools. Afterwards they would go and watch the whores dance at The Rag Doll on Nebraska Avenue. But like has been said, Kuka'd pass out. He was always careful not to do so until he got home. It was just something he felt strongly about.

He didn't like to get up before noon. He considered it bad luck. The only way to counter this was if he woke up early with a girl and started fucking. That way it would usually turn out right. He'd go buy a *Tribune* and throw away everything but the sports pages and comics. He'd drink Cuban coffee. After that he'd start drinking beer. Then he'd have some Tums. He'd smoke a reef. Later he'd take some speed because the beers would add up on him. After awhile his liver would start acting funny. You're not supposed to be able to feel your internal organs? he would question himself. He'd move about all afternoon doing things which were out of focus. Around sundown he'd sit on the porch and watch cars go by. He'd be just starting to really wake up. He had fallen in love with the night. When I die, he told his friends, I want you to bury me in the dark.

Every once in awhile, he would consider turning his life around. But he had tried to do that once and all that happened was, he hurt his shoulder. It was a life lived by chance. If he did anything right, he backed into it.

When he'd stay alone so much, he'd get paranoid. There was always a lot of shit in the house. Their whole stake. Good years of hard time if he got caught. There was that abandoned gas station across the street. Behind it was a little place, almost a dollhouse, that kids had played in once. It was locked up and empty inside. It was one room and had a little porch on the front of it that was painted green. Sometimes he would go over there and watch his own house. If he'd left the light on there, often it appeared to his imagination that he could see himself across the street. There was an easy chair on the porch of the dollhouse that moths had eaten the back out of. There was an old rusted glider. They were so run down no one bothered to steal them. He would sit on one of these in the dark. Across the street, he would see himself looking through the window wondering if anyone was out there.

# 6. BOSS-TOOTH

Sometime later that night, Wade came over to where Kuka was leaning against the wall. Wade usually had some character wanting to tell him one thing or another, like Emmett Pike, who was making his way toward them just now. Emmett had spent eleven months on river patrol in the Delta, then was sent home early with malaria. His eyes still had the jungle in them. Had vines in them, the vegetable smoke. So that Wade had told him finally, maybe about a year ago back, Look Deuce, you need to wear some dark glasses, man.

So Deuce had put on dark glasses, and he never took them off. Wade looked at him now: He had black hair, a thin, wiry little guy with a long neck and long face and a penciled-in mustache, kind of tough and ratty in appearance, and very pale, with big front teeth, one overlapping the other a bit. When he got fucked up like he was now, he'd shuffle around like an old man and mumble to where you barely understood him. When you saw him like that it was hard to believe he could shoot pool so accurately that sometimes hardened men would stand around the tables and rhapsodize about it. He was a hopeless and endearing sort, and Wade said to Kuka now, as Deuce shuffled toward them like a blind man, "He's crazy, that's all. Crazy as a shithouse rat." But they was all of them crazy. Those who insisted they weren't, you'd read about them later in the newspapers.

"Look," Deuce said. "I got it. Here's what we do. We get some grunts come in here with M-16's an' blow this shit away, ever' las' one a these assholes. 'Cept we save the pretty ones. Yeah. We save the pretty girls an' we fuck them. Then later on we push 'em down the steps. If we can find six pretty girls in here at any one time, we'll use 'em for pallbearers."

"We gone take any souvenirs?" Wade asked.

"We'll cut off their ears an' all their fingers an' toes an' their noses, too. If anyone comes behind us they won't be able to do nothin' but spit on 'em. Man, we gone count *coup*."

Or like Tommy Capshaw, the old boxer. Tommy'd been Middleweight Champion of the World, but that was years back, in the late '50's. Now he was a railbird.

"How much I owe you?" he asked Wade.

"Couple bucks."

"The merry-go-round," Tommy said. "It'll be startin' up...." He counted some of his fingers, then seemed to lose track of what it meant. "I got them ponies down. Say. I'm good for it."

Wade said: "Say."

Then they both made their shoulders jump, feinted their hands.

"Shit, Wade," Tommy said. "I'm faster'n 'at." Then ole Tommy, he smiled like a piano.

Or take Billy deGrace, who at the moment was sitting at the next table over, displaying his boot knife to a big, raw-eyed blonde.

Wade walked over to him.

"Billy, put that away."

The blonde got a little upset by the situation and spilled her drink.

"Damn, Wilma," said Billy deGrace, wiping the liquor off his blade. "I wish you hadn't a done that. It'll get drunk, an' later on it might cut me."

Now sometimes Wade would be a certain way, and he'd stay in it. But other times he'd fast deal his moods, one on top the other, always looking around like he was in a back alley. Or maybe he'd just stare.

Say here comes a punk. They'd come from miles around to get a shot at him. Wade would just look at him. But it went like this: *Fuck you, asshole. I don't give a shit. Go talk to the damned. Talk to 'em if they'll have you. This is fire, this ain't nothin' you drink of. Stand at a distance. Keep a hand on your keys. I don't lie. It's all here in black and white. An' don't even try to tell me nothin', you're too late. Gone. Tell the boys you stood up to Wade Bonner. An' take a grain of salt with you. You know God don't want a see you naked.*

Now if you got on the wrong side of him some way, you stayed there. Like this cowgirl that came up to him now. Wade'd been putting his spell on the room, copping that attitude such as he would.

"I swear," the cowgirl said, "you're the most selfish man." She cocked a hip, stood there like that. She had on a white leather jacket with fringe down the arms. "You jus' won't share yourself one bit." The words were plain, but she was saying it tough.

"Go on," Wade said. "Beat it."

Then she wanted to buy him a drink, but he don't drink.

"I jus' want to be your pal," she said finally. "You got no fight with me."

"How 'bout suckin' on this?" Wade said, and he juggled his balls a couple times.

"You're jus' tryin' to shock me."

"No. Yer wrong," he said. "I'm tryin' to make a fool out a you."

She was angry then. "Well, I'm leavin'!" she said. And Deuce, who's standing there rolling his eyes at all of this, pipes in, "So put down a deposit so we know you're serious."

After she went away, Kuka asked Wade, "What was that all about?"

"She made fun a the way I walk," he said.

Well Kuka had to smile at that, though maybe it didn't show. Because Wade's walk was a slow dance, a stroll. And whether he was in motion or not, he had all those moves going. He had more moves than anyone.

"'Do you remember me?' she asks me. Shit," Wade said. "I guess she forgot who she was and wanted me to remind her."

And those who got hooked on the moves, he already had them where he wanted. He'd leave them behind. The way he looked around somehow arranged the room. And if he couldn't keep it steady with his attitude, he knew the angles too, and how to shorten a ring. And he wouldn't leave his back blind, not ever.

But sometimes he didn't bring all this with him, and you saw that a big part of him was still a kid.

Those of you who knew him in the old days in Tampa before he passed into legend would know this was true, if he was a friend of yours, or if you was a woman, and he was your man for awhile.

# 7. O'NEIL CARTER'S LIVER PILL

O'Neil knew the names of all the animals and birds and plants. Sometimes he claimed that he could foretell the weather. He could quote the Bible well as any preacher, and he knew some of the old stories that'd never made it to the books.

Before O'Neil left that morning, Kuka, who had the shakes a little and didn't feel too hot in general, mentioned something about what alcohol was doing to his stomach.

"That ain't it," O'Neil said. "You jus' ain't recognized your poison." And he proceeded to tell a tale about a magic turtle.

"It was a monster," he said. "Either he was a cooter or alligator snapper, no one pinned it down. An' its food was human bein's. Because of it," O'Neil said, "the mockingbird lost its own voice, an' forever after was doomed to copy the songs of others.

"It had such power over stone and water, it could take any shape it pleased. An' being how only fishermen ever saw it in its true appearance—you see, it wouldn't show but if it was rainin' or times at dusk when the mosquitoes was all swarmed up—it was somewhat of a legend at the barbershop, but little known elsewhere.

"It was the first creature," O'Neil said, "to learn the knowledge of bridges. By the shape of its back, it crossed over anywhere it wanted. It could become invisible. It often appeared in the disguise of a little girl. The old men said that she talked with a lazy 's.' An animal of black-eyed beauty. Her eyes, they agreed, spoke for themselves, but it was all just a front...."

Now Kuka had taken on that weird, lost expression sheep get when they're being sheared.

"Is that true?" he asked.

"I shit you not," O'Neil said. "But listen up, it's like this—when it lived among people, no one knew its identity. And it went from place to place, killin' them when it needed food. When it was hungry, there were no survivors." And he added, "Well, almost none.

"Now the mockingbird made a deal with it, thinkin' that this was the Devil himself. I got no idea what it was they'd agreed on. Only thing, see, the Devil heard tell a this an' took retribution. He split the bird's tongue.

"But there were some people the monster liked. No one knows why." O'Neil looked off in a contemplative manner. Then he said, "Maybe it was in they resembled turtles in the face, or by their slow movements. I'm jus' not certain. But the ones it liked, it'd only eat their livers. That's why your stomach's goin' t'hell," O'Neil said. "You ought a consider yourself lucky. 'Cause you one a them it has a fondness for.

"The mockingbird," he said. "Listen to him now. He's mastered all the songs."

They grew quiet and listened.

# 8. A CLEAR CUT SIGN

When Kuka got back to the house with the pistol that morning, there'd been two messages on the door. One from Mickey's girlfriend, Johnnie. It was some kind of screen she was putting up. He couldn't figure what it meant at all. Mick'd already driven away, so he just crumpled it. The other was from Shay Carbonell. Come over, it said.

Kuka broke down the pistol and cleaned it. Then he couldn't get it back together right. The cylinder wouldn't line up. Any bullets come out a there, he thought to himself, they gonna get shaved. After awhile he said the hell with it and walked on down to Shay's. She lived on the Hillsborough River. The river was three blocks west of the bar. Then he went south five blocks. It was a pretty good walk.

Kuka'd owned a car once, but he couldn't keep up with it. In order to start the motor, he had to turn on the windshield wipers and lights and honk the horn before he turned the key.

When he turned off the ignition, the ashtray had to be full of cigarettes, or the car would keep running. Somebody hot-wired it one night at the bar. The car only made it a half block before it broke down. He'd sold it to John the Hat for fifty bucks.

Whenever he could, Kuka would stop under an oak and rest. Outside the shade, the day looked like it was about to burst into flames.

There was a long winding driveway to Shay's house. As Kuka walked down it, he came upon a decrepit garden with a scarecrow standing in it. There was something about the scarecrow that caught his eye. He went and stood before it awhile until he realized it had on one of his shirts.

All that was left of the garden were collard greens that had started to flower. The scarecrow too was run down. It had a flour sack for a face with black circles drawn on for eyes, and no mouth. It had on a red wig and old slouch hat with a hole in the crown. There was something of Harpo Marx to it, but the resemblance was faint.

Kuka said to it:

"Maybe you got some first hand knowledge a this, I don't know, but ... say the birds was gettin' out a hand. Take that mockingbird...." He listened as though he could hear its mad song in the distance. "Now I don't admire to say it, but it's my belief that bird is gone to seed. An' some the others, like that rooster what's jus' gotta crow ever' mornin' ... anybody'd keep a rooster in the city's cut from a selfish pattern to begin with ... well, there you are," he added, as if he had summed it all up.

"Now you ask me if anything is the matter ... I should say there was. Let me put it on the table for you ... an' it's like that ole girl told me once—you don't get it now, it's yer own damn fault."

Unaccustomed to so many words, he had begun to get drunk on them.

"Well it's a curiosity to nature how they get that way." The wind soughed through the collards. "It's somethin' ain't right. An' you heard the sayin'—the devil stirs the pot but forgets the lid? What it means is that trouble's easy to get into, but hard to cover up. You see what I'm gettin' at?" The scarecrow of course said little, and if anything, appeared quite stunned by the conversation.

"Now I'll bow my knee in some lonesome valley," he continued, "an' say my Our Father's and Hail Mary's an' recall me do's and don'ts, but what I'm for here is a clear cut sign. Like as to what side a the fence I'm settin' on. An' I hope it comes soon, I tell you, 'cause I'm startin' to feel like two cents waitin' for change...." He went on in this vein for several minutes before it became clear even to him that every time the narration took one step forward, it slipped back two. "An' that ain't no lie nor whore's dream," he finished up.

He looked at the scarecrow hopefully for a moment or two longer. Then he abandoned the whole line of thought and walked around to the back of the house.

Shay was sunbathing in the yard. Her people were from a country in Europe that no longer existed. She had oak-colored hair that was bobtailed and awkward. She was not pretty. She was beautiful in the manner a woman who isn't perfect finds a way to use her best features. And her body, Lord, it'd turn a man's eye.

They had only one thing in common, and Kuka brought that up. "Let's go to bed."

"That's not why I asked you over," she said. She was reading a popular magazine. There was a fashion model on the cover with an enormous mouth. "There's something I need."

Kuka said nothing. He didn't want to hear it.

Shay's backyard was an acre of land that stretched along the river. The owner of the property boarded some horses there. Kuka watched a red colt by the water in grass up to its belly. Suddenly it danced sideways.

"Besides," Shay said, "I have to teach ballet tonight."

"What's that got to do with it?" he said. "It ain't gonna take long."

She rolled over on her back. She had on a bikini bottom about the size of an eye patch, and nothing on top.

"Kuka, you wait just a minute, now. I know this is the sort a thing that brings out your primitive nature," she began.

"No, that ain't it. What I'm doin' is choking a chicken here, see. Look at the sonbitch's head."

"Let's go inside," she said. "What if my boyfriend comes around an' you got that out?"

Her house was nice. Small. A stone fireplace. The kitchen table by a window overlooking the river. And every once in awhile a horse would walk by and look in.

"How's the horses doin'?" Kuka said. He was just making small talk.

"I don't know," Shay said. "Why don't you go fuck one?"

"Look, I got shit on my mind," he said, "you got no idea about."

"Wait. Wait," she said. There was some opera on the radio. She went over and turned it up and started pirouetting very slowly.

"Kuka ... there's a possum living in the attic." She spun around like she was hooked to a treadle. "That crack in the ceiling ... he pisses through there onto the floor."

Kuka looked at the ceiling.

"He's tryin' to drive me nuts. He murdered a cat up there last night."

Just as Kuka was thinking, This is the biggest crock a shit I ever heard, there was a stirring overhead, and the possum unloaded through the rafters.

On his way back home, Kuka said to his mind: This all makes more or less no sense. Makes me kind a trust it. Then he saw the rooster-tail clouds building in the sky. O'Neil'd taught him they foretold a change in the weather.

# 9. THE KNIFE AND GUN CLUB

The name of the place was The Cadillac Bar. It was the kind of bar you'd go to early and forget to eat. You was kind of tough, or a little crazy, or you was in the process of hardening up. Or maybe some friends said they'd meet you here, but they ain't showed yet, and you're sitting at a table feeling somewhat out of place.

The people around you are thieves and whores, cowboys, bikers, off-duty cops—they're on parole, underage, they're all tricked out in their finest. Or say, look at the old lady with the bowling shirt on, her face expressing the sorrow of three widows.

And there's roughly a hundred of these refugees from the various generations revolving at different speeds around the bar area, stopping periodically to order a drink or to hallucinate in raw colors upon the shell-back telephone in the corner that rings through the night—but look, there ain't nobody here by that name.

And all inside this held motionless for a second as they pass through the strobe light, then canceled out into the blue smoky crowd, and the band playing honky tonk just a little out of key. It's so dark on the dance floor you can't imagine how sorry that girl is you just danced with, but she's all right in your book, because you had your hands all over it, and she said kind of hoarse in your ear, "You sure know how to move."

Or say later you're still there, and it's getting on toward the back-side of the evening. And having settled in under the weight of many beers, you're trying to extract some meaning from the random turn of events that brought you to this place—when all of a sudden, one of the characters you have perhaps dreaded meeting all your life enters the bar with two partners. And you say to your mind, just as everyone else has, That son of a bitch looks just like a bear.

And he did, too. He came in from the night sideways, one of them men you can't tell how tall they are. Say he was 350 pounds with a huge, burled head. He wagged his head several times in the dimness, stopped the first pretty girl he came to and laughed hysterically, which mortified all those who witnessed it. He took up two bar stools and commenced to eat pigs feet and red hots. He had on a brown T-shirt with a streak of salt down the back, had on what you call high-water pants. He was a fashion plate now. The crowd started talking about pitbulls and hogs.

And these two boys he had with him, they just stood around snapping their fingers and bluffing everyone. This one, a big cowboy, was a barrel his own self, and he looked like he was in shape. But the third one was kind of dark and thin, just scaffolding, a slide trombone of a man. And there were those who questioned whether or not he was but someone's shadow that'd gotten loose.

Time got a little strange about all this, like it had slowed down to take note.

"Only 30 minutes has passed by in the last hour," is how John the Hat explained it. John got his name not because he wore a hat, but that he had been to college once and fashioned himself a thinker.

Now just then the bear went and stood before a fat girl who wrestled at the Armory under the name Bovine Sweets. She had a tendency to take up with men who treated her badly. He lolled his head some and curled his lip in a mean way, and she understood somehow it as an invitation to dance.

And to tell the truth, they was cutting up out there. They danced like a pair of scissors. And here's his two partners going (snapping their fingers).

Well the boys were standing around chewing the fat about all this, being ironic how they will. Of those in attendance, Billy deGrace put it most eloquently.

"His breath'd knock a buzzard off a shit wagon," Billy said.

"I don't believe he was reared a Christian," Bullet threw in his two cents worth. Bullet was called so because he was absolutely the slowest man in town.

"I believe he was reared a animal," Deuce observed.

Sparky the waitress brought the boys their drinks then, and talking in that lazy way of hers, said about the bear:

"That's a double-wide now. A double-wide. Them two boys with him?"

To which John David Singletary replied:

"It looks to me they all came in the very same car." John David looked thoughtful for a moment and then summed it up to the boys' satisfaction.

"Basically," he said, "they are what you call a three-headed asshole."

# 10. THE FIGHT

There was a great deal of odd behavior that night. There was some slapstick early on to the right of the dance floor. The dance floor was small, it got rough sometimes. You could catch an elbow. "FUCK OFF!" somebody'd shouted at the end of a fast song. And you saw a beer bottle come down like a Ferris wheel upon his head.

It was some kind of carny undertone. A bunch of Nam boys were around, each of them in some kind of camouflage. It looked like a combat fashion show for awhile. This old guy had remarked, "Yeah. They the ones. They the ones you been read about. The ones didn't make it back. The M.I.A.'s." But it was like Wade said: "What's he know?"

After what they called their Belt-Buckle-Polishing Song, the band, a group named The Rounders, shut down for break, and Kuka and Wade went out to the parking lot for a smoke. Wade rolled a couple. Shortly thereafter, Connie the waitress came out. By the way she looked at Wade, Kuka guessed who he'd been with of late. Her younger sister was Johnnie, Mickey's girlfriend. Both of them was hard for Kuka to get a slant on. They had oversized eyes, something gypsy about them, bad teeth, and when they moved, their breasts swang. They're trouble, is what would cross his mind. He told this to Wade one time, and he said, "Yeah ... but that's what I'm lookin' for, is trouble." Connie was speed-nodding a little, sexy like a cat what can't quite stay awake.

She started saying how nice the beach was, they'd been over to Indian Rocks, but Kuka looked at her and at Wade and neither one of them a lick of sun anywhere, and he understood that she was talking about the beach in a general sense. They were standing there not saying much but laughing some because the reef they had was amusing.

John the Hat came by then with this girl in a purple dress who'd been crossing her legs for the band. She hadn't been overly shy about it, whereby the drummer finally had brought a flashlight up on stage to get a clearer look. She had some nice pins on her too, but her face was short on pretty. Everyone at the bar knew by now that she didn't have no underclothes on, and it was a bit of a scandal among the women. From time to time she'd had the whole enchilada out. She had the hots for the singer, she'd been bird-dogging him for awhile, but he could give a shit. Maybe he'd given her a tumble one night, it wasn't ever clear. It was like she'd go around asking, "Is he mad at me?" And people are thinking, "No, he doesn't even remember you." So John the Hat ended up with her, how he'd do. John was one of the first of those who didn't go to Viet Nam to prove you could catch Post Stress Syndrome from your friends. He was a little dinky-dow, see.

As they were walking up, Kuka said to Wade:

"She ain't much to look at, but I like her attitude."

But Wade was looking past him.

"There's our boy," he said.

The bear and his partners were leaning on a pickup across the parking lot. They were clowning it up. Someone walking by mentioned in passing that he really was an animal, no shit. And John the Hat retorted, "There is a closeness between his eyes that can't be explained in human terms."

Then John commenced to tell a story about when he was living up in Washington state and an Indian there had been arrested for sodomizing a bear. Now the girl in the purple dress either had a hearing problem or more likely was just about dumb as an oyster, but it was clear she hadn't quite come up to level on it.

"What the hell's wrong with a Indian?" she said finally. It was sort of a mysterious question, but John the Hat fielded it.

"There ain't," he said. "What's wrong with sodomizing bears?"

"Well, I don't know," she said kind of huffy. "Nothin' I guess. Long as you eat 'em."

Some eyes rolled on that, and John the Hat said, "Honey, come over here behind the dumpster, let's see what comes up."

Now Kuka had brought the pistol along with him. It was hidden in the back room in a paper sack. But he got to thinking on it and said:

"Wade ... that pistol comes into play tonight, might be best jus' wave the son of a bitch around some. Anybody fires it gone get their hand shaved." And he explained why. "I meant to tell you earlier," he said, "but that thought jus' totally fell out a my head."

Wade smiled.

"It fell out yer head?"

"Yeah."

"We don't need it," he said. "They ain't armed. Deuce seen to it."

Connie had added up what was happening here, and she asked:

"How you gonna handle this?"

But Wade just looked at her blank in the eyes and smiled again.

Kuka knew how he'd like to handle it. He'd heard it explained a time or two.

*Mostly it's just you get a hold of the guy as you can, when he ain't looking preferably, and slam him up against something real hard, kind of take his balance away. Then you got him at a disadvantage. The harder the object you throw him against, the more impact you have on his consciousness.*

Wade started saying then what was to happen to Cecil once he got out of jail or just as soon as he could take it up with him. It was a blood debt he was speaking of. And he concluded as follows:

"Ain't no use fuckin' around. Man does you wrong once, you can bet he'll do it again, jus' to remind you. Mark my word, Cecil 'll regret it till the day he dies ... if he lives that long."

When he talked that way and got that threat about him, the dark flash to his eyes, he became almost electrical in presence. It burned away the fear of those around him. But now he was talking about the fight like it was already over.

"When we put these assholes down, we jus' leave 'em where they lay. Yeah. That's good. See, because the longer they stay out, then when they come to, they won't even know their fucking names."

Well as he was saying this, here comes the bear shuffling that way. His two partners are a couple steps behind, just pure nonchalance, you understand.

"You ready for this?" Wade said.

"I don't see no way around it," Kuka replied.

"I ain't worried on the big one. He won't be able to get out his own way. The cowboy, though, that's a different story. The other one is of no consequence. He's got a skinny neck."

Now the bear got squared off, made his nose growl a couple times, and asked Wade:

"What're you doin'?" And they got into a staring contest right then.

"I'm mindin' my own bidness," Wade said. "What you doin'?"

"I'm wantin' a toke a that reef," the bear grumbled.

Wade took another hit. Thought for a moment or two on it. Said, "No."

Now even to a hardass such as this, it must have dawned somewhere that he'd come across a man who just did not give one shit. Or maybe he'd glanced into Wade's eyes just then, for they were insane and impossible to look at. But he kind of grunted and backed off a step or two, and made a joke with his boys.

In the meantime, Wade whispered to Connie, "Go get Mickey." They'd seen him earlier in Deuce's car selling ladies' watches.

Now after Connie'd gone off, Wade said to the bear:

"You know, there weren't but one pretty girl in this whole damn parkin' lot, and you done run her off."

Mickey came sidling around the corner then, listing this way and that. He took in the scene, looked once briefly at Wade, and a knowledge passed between them.

"Excuse me all t'hell," Mick said, like he was just passing through, and he slipped around behind the bear. And the bear's partners, they didn't seem to notice this, the fact their boy was set up. Down the line, Kuka saw Deuce leaning on a car. He had his black leather case out on the hood. He was studying the heavy end of his cue stick.

Time started stuttering and blinking then. Because all of a sudden the bear bowed up and punched Wade in the mouth. Then Mickey jumped on the bear's back and bent him over, and Wade struck with a right. The bear spun around from the blow, dropped against the hood of the car, right over the hood, Mick still on his back, and he comes off the hood and turns—Mickey like a rag doll on the back of a bear—and the man goes, "Arrrrrrrrrh," raises his hands over his head and starts running at Wade, Mick flung around like he's nothing there, and Wade thinks out loud, "O shit, I made him mad."

And he hit the bear as he's coming in, the right storming out of nowhere, caught him square with the hand stolen from the gods long ago in Babylon and passed from father to son, father to son. And the bear's weight and Mickey's weight falling into Wade, but he stepped aside, and the bear went right on down.

Then all a sudden, damn if he don't start to get back up. He's vertical but standing on his knees, come up for air to a world that was shifting before him. Then Mickey over him, six, seven hard shots to the face, each one making an angry cut.

But even before this, the cowboy's got his hands around Wade's throat, has him against the car, has leverage, and Wade's all but lifted off the ground. Then Kuka hit the cowboy twice square in the temple— bounced two rights off his head, and he didn't even seem to notice. And suddenly Kuka got spit out of the affair, like he'd fallen back into the normal sequence of the world, him just standing there cussing and shaking his goddamn hand. The cowboy had a hard head, now that's the truth.

He saw the bear down, choking in a pool of blood. Thought: Might have a body count there. He saw the dude with the skinny neck, down too, and having a hard time getting back on board. He'd tried to shag, but Deuce'd been in his way. Deuce was staring at his efforts now, bemused, chewing gum.

The bar had emptied out, and there's a crowd. Wade always could draw a crowd. It changed shape, backed away when the fight neared it. For awhile Wade and the cowboy are tangled up so on the ground nobody could hardly tell what is what. Then Wade had him in a headlock and banged his head against the fender of a car. Banged it again, and they broke apart. When Kuka saw this he noted to himself—This's over.

And sooner than the cowboy reckoned, that left of Bonner's hooked to his jaw. The cowboy looked like he'd bumped against the very world. He just hadn't expected quite so much. His eyes rolled up in his head, and he assumed that lost expression found on Queer Street. He kind of floated off to the left, and on down. Wade hit him so hard the cowboy pissed himself.

Then it was like it always was. Kuka'd seen this, now. Because Wade was on that high he got from fighting—ripping his shirt off, dancing around, "Who wants me—who wants me, come on ya sons a bitches...." He's all but sparking, and the pretty girls hanging on his arms, trying to get his feet back on the ground. Yeah. He loved that.

Later, after it was all done, Kuka heard one of the ladies of the night walking by:

"I don't care what nobody says," she confided to her companion. "That Wade Bonner's a Cobbtown sport."

That night the weather broke. It rained. And in the morning everything was cool.

## 11. FEEDING MONEY TO THE LAMBS

The next weekend, on a Sunday night, Wade got off work and went to the diner for breakfast. The bar closed early on Sundays. It was 1:30 a.m., maybe going on 2. Little Laura waited on him. Laura had worked at the bar for a time until she got sick of it, and before that she was a circus performer. She was 4' 7" tall and nearly as wide, and her hair was kind of tom-cat yellow.

"How's the pastrami sandwich look?"

"We ain't got no pictures," she said.

"How's the goulash?"

She regarded him. She looked him up and down.

"It's not for you," she said. "C'mon, wha'd you want?"

But she already knew what he wanted because he ordered the same thing every time.

So he got his steak and eggs and started to cover them up with Tabasco Sauce the way he would. He maintained it woke up the food.

But he had a problem on his mind. Something odd happened at work the past two nights. Patrol cars had started coming into the parking lot. The cops hassled people standing around. This hadn't ever happened before. It was unheard of. Wasn't that Shorty had the police paid off or nothing, but he was on good terms with them. And two, three of them would come in there when they was off-duty to drink. Everybody knew who they were, and didn't nobody care. They came in, got quietly shit-faced, then went home. They were good customers.

Well he was thinking on this, and sort of absently taking note of the diner patrons at the counter on the chrome-legged stools, when lo and behold if one of the city's finest don't set down opposite him in the booth with a cup of coffee. And he starts chatting.

Wade had never seen this particular cop before. Yet the man is familiar, it turns out, with many names from the bar. Then he shifted the conversation—if that's what it could be called, since Wade wasn't exactly talking at all—to when Bonner was prize fighting. He'd seen the Joe Roman bout at the Armory.

It'd tended to get on Wade's nerves, hearing his life spoken by a stranger. And he wasn't in for any take it seems, nothing easy like that you could figure. Rather it was a warning of some kind, and no specifics mentioned, just a little small talk to make it known that unseen eye was still around.

Truth be told, the cop had been awfully nice. The only unpleasantry occurred at the end of the conversation, and it came from Wade.

"You hadn't got yer eye fucked up, you was goin' places," the cop said. "Might a hit the big-time." He talked in that Tampa twang. When Wade didn't answer, the cop said, "What you think?"

Wade stopped his fork about half way to his mouth, gave him that look kind of arrogant and brooding and said, "I think I'm tryin' to eat here."

After he left, Wade asked Laura:

"You ever seen him before?"

"He comes in ever' now an' then. I don't know his name. He always leaves a good tip."

"You got that right," Wade said.

There was some discussion early that morning between Wade and Kuka about whether or not they might just ought to leave town. It was a means they'd practiced before, but now Tampa is a hard place to get out of. It has this strange pull to it. They did, however, decide to move.

Roy L.'s uncle had a garage apartment on Emma Street he'd been trying to sell for months. It was ten, twelve blocks south of where they'd been staying. "He'll rent you this place till he unloads it," Roy L. informed them about noon the next day. They got it for $175 a month.

Earlier in the week, Wade's gear had turned up at the bar. There it was one night outside the door when he came to work. Kuka thought once again, Say, Madonna's all right. But Wade, he just started looking through it make sure nothing was missing.

Didn't either of them have many possessions as such, except for Wade's barbells. What they owned fit in their duffel bags. So they packed their clothes and whatnot and were out of the old place by that evening, left the key on the dresser like they'd been staying at a motel.

The next couple days they got rid of their cache. After they squared their debts, Kuka's share came to five bills. They were out of business. This accomplished, Wade disappeared for a couple days.

Kuka spent some time checking out the neighborhood. It was the kind of area you might hear gunshots various nights. But otherwise it looked that you could be what you liked there, and do what you pleased. There was a pool hall a block away on Florida Avenue, and many young ladies walking the streets who seemed to had lost their dates.

Far as Kuka was concerned, getting a regular job was out of the question. It took up too much time and never paid anyways. John the Hat had explained to him once how the American working man was just like Robin Hood in reverse—that they stole from themselves to give to the rich. It was one of the few things John ever said that made any sense, and Kuka added it to his store of knowledge. He figured he'd have a month to come up with something, though what that might be offered no clues whatsoever. He decided to put it out of his mind.

In so doing, he got seriously trashed at several bars that night. He spent a croaker accomplishing this, and exactly what he got for his money was unclear in the morning. He remembered that he'd gone to a club and seen Johnnie Blue and The Nightmares play, but that's about all he was certain of. He wondered if he'd dropped a twenty, or if a barmaid hadn't pulled a shuffle with his change. But he often wondered things such as this, and they were never true.

He did determine, though, somewhere in the night, that what he needed was an occupation such as Wade's. For the most part, his job consisted of dancing with what pretty girls come in the bar, or else he was out in the parking lot sampling the latest imports. Any way Kuka looked at this, it beat working 40 hours a week in a machine shop or what have you, where he might get his fingers bobbed, or worse, some joker would make him work overtime and act like he was doing this as a favor.

Thursday morning, Kuka walked down to the paper machine to get a *Tribune*. He put his money in and took out a paper, turned to the sports pages and started reading "The Morning After" column by Tom McEwen. While he was doing this, Bud Garza pulled over to the side of the street in his wrecker.

They talked.

Buddy was a mechanic. He was a regular at the bar, during the daytime at least. He was married and had three kids. He also had a wild streak he'd let run from time to time. And that evening when he got off work, the two of them went to a pub in the north end.

Buddy didn't have much cash on him, so Kuka sported him some drinks. But now Kuka, as the night wore on, got to thinking about that bar. They ended up staying there until they got hustled out at closing time, which was 1 o'clock, it being a beer and wine joint. By then maybe there was them, two waitresses and a couple college kids, a derelict, and a cook with a dwarf hand.

Kuka'd never been there before. They didn't know him from Adam. And he got to mulling it over—what if he come busting in there late with a big hat pulled down over his ears, popped a cap or two into the ceiling and lifted the night's take?

They were sitting at a booth by a window that was back lighted by the bar sign outside. There was a potted plant by the window where Buddy spit his tobacco juice. He looked like he had a baseball in his cheek. He had a long, narrow face, with a hooked nose, black-rimmed glasses and a downturned mouth. Because of his mouth, even when he was in good humor, he didn't necessarily appear to be. His clothes were all grease and oil. A fan blew the smell of onions down the bar as Kuka related his plan.

Buddy frowned. He wore a ballcap on his head backwards, catcher-style. He took it off and ran his forearm across his black hair in a sweeping motion. Then he put the hat back on.

Kuka modified his plan.

Buddy wiped his glasses off on a napkin, pointed the glasses off toward the light and squinted through them. He spit toward the planter. Sometimes during the evening he hit it, sometimes not. Finally, he spoke.

"You even got a gun?"

Kuka said, "It ain't worth nothin'."

"You got a car?"

"I don't," Kuka said.

"You kind a shit out a luck then, far as I can tell."

"How 'bout you helpin' me?" Kuka asked.

The only answer he got to this was in that Buddy ordered two more beers from a barmaid who was passing by. And when he started talking again, he seemed to have shifted the conversation entirely.

"I took my kids to the Lowry Park Zoo Sunday," he said. "They had some lambs there, you know, what the kids can pet an' shit. An' this one asshole, he was feedin' money to the lambs. Dollar bills. This was an adult. A grownup. The lambs was jus' eatin' up his dollar bills. I mean, lambs are pretty dumb, I guess...."

Then it was time to leave. And Buddy didn't say nothing else till they got back to Emma Street.

"Bud-ro," Kuka said then. "What you think?"

"'Bout what?"

"On what I was talkin' 'bout at the bar."

"I'll tell you what I'll do," he said. "You help me with a job, I'll get you a gun. A good one. A five, six hundred dollar piece. All you gotta do is drive. It'll be easy. I don't come back in a certain amount of time, you drive the car back to the shop an' park it. So you covered all around. That way, you'll have a gun at least. You can use it or sell it or what have you. But I can't help you with no stick-up. Maybe it sounds okay, I ain't sayin'. Though personally, for me, there's too many variables. I got a family to support. I can't take a fall."

The next morning, Kuka went down to Buddy's garage. It was just a garage where people hung around kicking tires and such. At noon, Buddy locked the place up. He picked out one of his customer's cars, a late model Olds, and changed the plates on it. He had Kuka drive up to Temple Terrace, to an older subdivision by the river. He had put on a dark suit. He had gloves. A big, leather briefcase. A hat like the old guys wear in the black and white movies. He looked like maybe he was in the neighborhood hawking cemetery plots.

They stopped once at a pay phone so Buddy could make a call. He talked in Spanish.

"Who'd you call?" Kuka asked.

"My brother, Hilario," Buddy said. "He's our alibi, jus' in case. Right now," he looked at his watch, "we're eatin' lunch with him at Latams on Columbus Drive."

"Hilario," Kuka said. "That the crazy one?"

"No," Buddy said, "that's Picot."

Kuka thought for awhile. He said, "What we havin' for lunch?"

"Boliche," Buddy said. "Moros ... yucca. It's the special today."

A couple minutes later Kuka said, "Bud-ro."

"Yeah."

"Let's get some them fried bananas, too."

Buddy turned and gave Kuka a sidelong glance, raised his eyebrows and shook his head once as if to clear it, then looked back to the road.

Finally they found the street Buddy wanted, and Kuka dropped him off. He drove down to a 7-Eleven and got a couple beers, then picked Buddy up at the same spot he'd left him. Now the briefcase looked to be loaded with rocks. Later on, when they opened it at the garage, he had maybe three, four grand worth of pistols and ammo.

"This prick used to come to the shop an' get his car worked on. Always bitched on the job I did. You couldn't please 'im. So the last time he does this, I jus' tell 'im, 'Hey, fuck you. Don't come 'round no more.' But he'd bring these guns in here, an' be braggin' on his collection. An' I jus' filed that piece a information away.

"I didn't get all of it. Jus' the expensive shit."

Kuka took a snub-nosed Ruger Speed-Six Magnum with a rubber combat stock.

Buddy gave him a box of hollow points.

"Wait a minute," he said. "Take these instead," and he handed over a box of factory load.

"Them holla points got a muzzle flash at night, damn near blind you."

## 12. IN THE CAN

The place on Emma Street was a small, two-story building that made a corner on the block. They took the top apartment. Wooden steps climbed up the left side of the building to their door. Friday evening, an hour before Wade had to go to work, he and Kuka sat on the top step.

Wade was always singing to himself, listening to some music that wasn't playing out loud. He had on blue jeans, a black T-shirt, his jumpboots. They were looking at the Ruger. When Wade held it, the weapon seemed smaller. He had big hands and wrists.

"You need to go see Dorsey," he was saying to Kuka. "Tell him we can't buy no more shit for awhile." He said, "Don't tell nobody where we moved to. No one."

"I'll go see Dorsey tomorrow," Kuka said.

Then Wade got talkative. He'd do that sometimes with Kuka.

"It was weird at the bar last night," he said. "Jus' one them nights. This one motherfucker's in there, an old guy, an' he's plastered. He goes and sits down with people at their tables, you know ... like a couple's settin' at a table havin' a nice time, here he comes. Sets down an' starts fuckin' with 'em. Wants to strike up a conversation, or whatever. But he's so fucked up you can't understand what he's sayin' even. An' he's old, somebody's gramps, for Christ sake. So I don't want a be hardass with him, I'm jus' tryin' to get him out a there.

"After awhile I take him outside to look for his car. We lookin' all over for it. Then 'bout ten minutes later he remembers he didn't drive there—he took a cab. God! This fucker's drivin' me nuts by now. So I call a cab. An' the cabby comes—I don't see this now—the cabby comes, an' they'd some feud earlier or some shit, but he comes in, takes one look at the old guy an' flattens him. Knocks him cold. An' I don't see this. All I see is, I see the cabby leavin'. Hey, I tell him, Wait, yer fare's over here. Hey, the guy's in here. You gonna leave him or what? The guy keeps turnin' around goin', you know, Fuck you. He's wavin' with his arm—get out a here. Like he thinks I'm bein' a smart ass, bein' funny about it or something ... an' this sets the tone for the whole night."

Well they were sitting there on the steps laughing about this, when a guy comes walking by across the street.

"Check this out," Kuka said. "It's the third time I've seen him. Same get-up."

He was dressed like a biker, in the colors of a gang, but he didn't have no bike anymore or something. He'd just walk around the neighborhood with his helmet on. He passed by them, tall, walking a little too erect, his eyes hard-wired into the distance up ahead.

"One of our finer citizens, I'm sure," Wade said. He watched him some more. "Damned if he don't look like that buddy a mine, Bohannon. This dude I met in the can there at Ft. Bragg.

"You know they had some bad fucking niggers there. Shit ... they was bad. But I never got nothin', I mean maybe in a couple scraps and what not, but I never got my ass kicked. Nobody ever *got* me. But they fucked up some people good.

"There was one crazy dude named Bulldog—a white boy. This guy's a fool, now. Didn't have no brain. He's from Georgia I think. Somewhere. But he's always be talkin' 'bout these niggers. It was when this Sergeant John Law was there. That was his real name. A great big ole spade, an' I mean this guy was tough, didn't take no shit and didn't take no sides either. I seen him throw a bunch a large black bodies around for a number of minutes one time, an' I thought—This guy's not on anybody's side, he's gonna get 'em all! An' he's in charge of us, see.

"There's this one real mean red-headed nigger who's wearin' a neck brace. We're outside gettin' ready for formation or somethin', an' Bulldog says out loud, you know, loud enough so's everybody around there can hear, says about the red-headed nigger, 'He looks like one them statues my mama used to have in the front yard.' God! But Sergeant Law shuts everybody up right now. The niggers gonna pay attention to him 'cause he can whip 'em all. He kept 'em from doin' anything ... but later, they beat Bulldog's ass, I mean ... but he's so damn dumb, it don't even make an impression.

"I'll never forget my buddy there, Bohannon. An Irishman, so we get along right away. He's cool. An' me an' him got on good. Then one day the niggers took to beatin' the fuck out him. Consistently, day after day. An' after awhile Bohannon became very interested in cuttin' everybody's hair, combing their mustaches. Shit. I couldn't believe it. Gonna get everybody trimmed up. Always tryin' to keep his hands real clean.

"One day, Bulldog—see, the niggers was beatin' up on the white guys, so we was always tryin' to get together an' form a gang of our own ... like if they see a bunch a white guys standin' around together, they gonna pick one an' beat hell out him, 'cause they figure you tryin' to make an uprisin'—so Bulldog—there's six, eight of us together in the middle of this meetin' we're havin', layin' plans for the big revolution—Bulldog says, 'Fuck it, we ought a start it right now, jus' like this!' An' he runs out into the hallway an' says, 'Come on you fuckin' niggers!'

"Nuts. The guy's jus' fucking nuts. So about ten niggers jumped on him an' kicked the living shit out a him. We all jus' stood there, like—I don't believe this...." His voice trailed off. "Yeah. The revolution took on a quieter tone after that. Then half of 'em quit, and the other guy stopped comin'.

"Now the baddest dude was named Ivory. This big spade. Tall dude. One time I'm in the messhall on K.P. an' he had somethin' to say to me. He's there at the window where you put your tray in there to get it washed. Well he's gettin' ready to put his tray in there, an' he stopped. I'm behind him, an' now he's holdin' me up. An' he knows he's holdin' me up. So I'm jus' gonna stop an' wait. Hey, I'm in the can, you know, what am I, in a hurry? So he jus' stood there an' waited, an' he don't say nothin', an' I don't say nothin'. Dumb. I mean. Jus' really fucking dumb, the whole thing. So then he says real loud, he's talkin' to the whole messhall now, 'FUCKIN' WHITE BOYS 'ROUND HERE TRYIN' T'MAKE YOU HURRY UP!'

"I jus' mumble under my breath, 'Fuck you.' He says, 'Wha'd you say, white boy?' An' I start screamin', FUCK YOU! FUCK YOU!' I threw my tray down an' shit. Went fucking loony on 'im.

"But they got respect for a crazy white man. They really do.

"One time this spade gives me a haircut. You know he's just a spade, he ain't one the violent blacks, the ones were doin' all the mangling of bodies, threw one motherfucker out a second-story window an' shit, so I ain't worried 'bout him, I ain't even thinkin' about him. He'd chop off a little piece here, a little piece there, an' I don't even notice. I'm not payin' attention. I don't know this guy's makin' a fool out a me. So I get my haircut, put on my hat an' walk out. But when I took my hat off later, everybody fucking went nuts. It's a big joke, see?

"But so you know who wants to cut my hair right? Bohannon. Yeah. 'That's okay,' he says, 'I'll fix yer hair, come on.' An' he kept goin' on an' on with it. He took so long cuttin' it, I'm goin', 'Come on, Bo,' I'm sayin', 'Just get done with it.'

"An' he became very interested in that kind a shit. The poor guy. Poor Bohannon. They stumpbroke him. They'd jus' beat the fuck right out a him...."

# 13. DORSEY WILLIAMS

The tin-roofed, yellow house on a side street in Belmont Heights, in a neighborhood of old, small houses, looked the same—the roof piled high with pine needles, the same ladder leaning against one side where Dorsey, once years ago under a vow of sobriety which did not last the entire day, had begun to scrape paint. But there were too many cars around, in the yard, along the curb, large Chryslers, station wagons, and other assorted sleds.

Kuka paid the cabby.

Dorsey was sitting in a lawn chair on the front porch—this little guy who was otherwise skinny but somewhat wide at the belt. He had a white beard, a square face, his hair in cornrows. He appeared kind of dressed-up for him, a string tie, his clothes clean and pressed, though he wore his old butterscotch house slippers.

He looked done in. He glanced at Kuka once, then shied away.

Dorsey pulled himself up slowly, padded noiselessly across the wooden floor, motioning for Kuka to follow him. Neither one of them spoke.

The inside of Dorsey's house was crowded with fish tanks. Every wall space taken by them. The house a little bit like low tide. Kuka gandered at some of the tropicals as he walked in, but quickly then a little circle of spades, four women and two men, caught his eye. They were in the living room all but knitted together.

"What's up?" Kuka said.

Dorsey just shook his head. He took Kuka into the living room and introduced him around: Opal, Laveda, Hodgret, Yolanda, Robert and Dexter. They were all dressed to the nines. Fish in the big tanks behind them seemed to fall lazily down the air.

Dorsey walked to the kitchen, and Kuka followed. Here Dorsey hatched brine shrimp and prepared his formulas to feed the thousands of fish he owned. He broke a little then. He took out a bottle of pills from a cabinet and downed a couple.

"World ain' so cold behind some red."

There was a quart of Lord Calvert on top of the icebox. He took it down. Hit a good one from the bottle. "Log Cabin help, too," he said. He took another, much healthier shot, winced hard, and after this second one said, "I sure needed that one." He looked at Kuka and added somewhat distractedly, "I had enough fo da time bein'."

But he'd been at it already, his words stumbling around. Kuka glanced back to the living room. The women were crying. Some of them were praying. The one making the biggest commotion strongly resembled a man in the face.

"C'mon," Dorsey said.

They headed toward the back porch. Dorsey stopped at a side door and opened it. In that room a wino sat on an orange couch. He was old and black, and he was eating a hard-boiled egg. He was surrounded by bottles of liquor and wine and a cooler full of beer and so much meat and fruit it looked like a feast for many people. The wino seemed to be trashed to the point of contemplation. He was frowning at the egg. Dorsey closed the door.

He said, "Dey took 'im out. Took 'im out de here an' now."

Kuka regarded him, and though half not wanting to know, he asked: "What you sayin'? You tell me right now."

"You wan' see 'im?" Dorsey said. "Cain't 'member if you ever meet mah nephew, Laf...."

On the screened-in back porch there was a young man laid out in a casket. Behind him were the big breeder Black Angels Dorsey was known for. At a slant to this, another tank held Dorsey's piranha. The tanks were huge. The piranha swam near the young man's left ear.

Kuka stared at the dead man. He was laid out in a cream colored three-piece linen slack suit. He had a pensive and somewhat varnished look about him.

"Laugh?" Kuka said.

"Yeah. Laf ... is short for Lafayette."

Dorsey started again: "Tore 'im down. He look fine, though, don't 'e?"

Kuka thought, That's the grayest lookin' nigger I ever seen in my life.

"He al'ays on ugly side de family ... cain't do nothin' 'bout that. Al'ays too young in de mind, too. You knows the kind I'm sayin'—not too sitiated, don't know where ever'thang at? One his pool hall associates over a bet dey had. Lord ...it cain't gets no worse, i's got to get better." He looked at his nephew and scoffed, "Honky-tonk man, you know.

"He ugly as sin, ain' 'e? I ain't goin' lie to you. But long on style. He could dress hisself all right. Don't know if you ever saw like dis before— to wake 'em at home." He turned a hand over, palm up. "Laf al'ays remind a you a little ... jus' sompin goofy wid 'im ...." The hand moved like it was doing the talking.

Kuka took a deep breath. He looked through the window screen to the backyard. The backyard was crowded with fish tanks made from the insides of refrigerators. The water in them was green.

"Ain't no birds here," he said finally, as if this had some bearing on anything.

"Shit ... ain' no bird ... jailbird here is all. I's cold. An' you couldn't tell 'im nothin'. Hard to get over to. His daddy took it bad. But he stronger 'n his mama—she mah sister, Hoddy. She might never come back from it. Let his bad friends overtake 'im."

A five minute, incomprehensible monologue followed, after which he said, "Dat's it in a nutshell," and suddenly focused on Kuka again as if just then aware of his presence.

"Wha'd you here for?"

Kuka said, "Me an' Wade got this shitstorm comin' our way. Can't buy no more goods for some time. We'll get back to you soon's we can."

Dorsey waved his hand, brushing this off.

"I can pick up de slack," he said. "You go on now. I got shit I got a think on. I might have to drink hard liquor behind it. My mind's too keen. Gone wid chu ... 'fore it get dark. An' don't dally on the streets, there's a meanness about. You ain't gone pass for no local. Gone. I ain' got time to stop an' chat, much as I long to."

He nodded toward Lafayette, said, "Be mindful a them close by ... a frien' have d'mos' access a hurtin' you. Don't wan' you end up a used-to-be."

As they walked past the wino's room the door was open then, and Kuka said:

"Who the hell is that?"

"He a sin-eater," Dorsey said. "All dat food an' drink—i's Laf's sins dere. Sin-eater gone eat all his sins away directly."

The wino had a pear in his hand. He did not appear to want to eat it. He was just studying it for some reason.

"I jus' cain't abide a fruits," Dorsey said.

When the cab picked Kuka up it was 5:30. The spades on East Lake Avenue were assembled on their porches and stoops to watch rush hour traffic. Laundry sailed from lines tied between buildings. Kuka looked at the naked yards.

"You my last fare out a here," the cabby said. "Be dark soon. Dark brings out the worst in this place. A damn jungle at night. They ought jus' well break out the fuckin' drums."

Kuka wasn't listening exactly. He was thinking back. He'd been at Ft. Campbell, Kentucky, when Otis Redding died. All the blacks took the day off. The whole post shut down. And he didn't get it. He's walking around, and the place is all but deserted. He's thinking, What's goin' on?

Finally he'd walked into a room, and there was a whole bunch of blacks there. And he sat down and smoked some dope with them, and they said, "You know, Otis Redding died today." "I'll be damned," Kuka said. And even then it didn't dawn on him—that the whole entire Ft. Campbell, Kentucky, closed down because of the fact Otis Redding died.

Kuka said, "You like drivin' cab?"

"Why?" the cabby said.

"I was thinkin' 'bout takin' a job."

"This ain't no line a work to be gettin' into," he said. "You gotta be fuckin' nuts drive a cab."

# 14. C. A. JONES

That Monday, Kuka went to see Charlie Tucker. Charlie worked in a shoe store down on 7th Avenue in Ybor City, Tampa's old Latin district, and the heart of the town.

He'd been doing this since high school, and he pretty much ran the place. How Kuka knew Charlie was in that Charlie's half brother, Vernon Swart, was some kind of shirt-tail relative to Deuce. It's all hard to trace. Charlie was half Cuban. His mother was one of them Cuban women who have a liking for Cracker men. Charlie still lived with her. His mother was totally nuts. Compared to her, Charlie was a piker—but that's another story entirely.

Charlie his own self wasn't no shining light. He was somewhat a fat slob. Like as if you was to give him a ride in your car, when he got in at the curb, the door would be hopelessly pinned to the ground.

His Cuban blood showed the most in him—big eyes, black curly hair, dark arms, he was horny as a toad. The reason Kuka went to see him now is that Charlie always had something going on the side. He knew about jobs not found in the newspapers, say. Far as easy money went, Charlie Tucker was sort of a very small-time alchemist.

A bell like on a Popsicle truck sounded off when Kuka opened the door of the shoe store. At that particular moment, Charlie appeared to all but have his head up a lady's dress. He was measuring her. He was working alone as usual. Kuka looked around at the latest styles, smelled the new leather, looked at his feet in the x-ray machine, and so forth until Charlie was done with his customer.

"She was showin' it to me, Kuka. Sideburns."

"Yer sick, Charlie." The lady looked like somebody's grandma.

"Hey ... what?" He's studying Kuka's boots in disgust. "Fucking antiques ... let me put some mink oil on 'em. Otherwise, they gone turn tough."

"I got somethin' else on my mind," Kuka said. "I'm lookin' for some cash money."

Charlie thought on that.

"Let me get it straight," he said flatly. "I trust we ain't discussin' no loan."

"No," Kuka said. "I'm talkin' about cash in general. Folding money."

Another customer came in—a young Latin woman, and she had on a bright yellow dress. It was so yellow you felt almost like you needed to get in the shade pretty soon.

"This bitch comes in every week," Charlie said to Kuka. "Her an' her wardrobe mean a lot to each other." Charlie sighed and groaned and farted and went to wait on her. He got her seated in his special chair. There was an intricate set-up of mirrors arranged about it. He could look up her dress from five angles. Kuka noted that she had a big ass, and wore her skirt tight against it.

"That's quite a yellow dress," Charlie said to her in Spanish. "You can all but get a tan from that."

He drew a blank. She looked at him real bored.

He said to Kuka across the aisle: "This chick's nowhere."

Kuka looked at Charlie, then at the girl.

"She don't speak English?"

"Not much," Charlie said. "How's it goin' anyways? I ain't seen you for awhile."

"Same shit," Kuka answered.

Charlie went to the back room to get some shoes. While he was gone, Kuka noticed that the Latin girl was staring at him.

They started trying on shoes. She said something to Charlie in Spanish. He answered. It was obvious they was talking about Kuka. "C. A. Jones," was all that he caught. The two of them started laughing.

"What's goin' on?" he said.

"She wanted to know who you were. I told her you was C. A. Jones."

Kuka looked at him. "I don't get it," he said.

"C. A. Jones ... *cajones*, you know."

"What's that mean?"

"Jesus, Kuka." Charlie was looking at him in disbelief. "You really do have to work at it, don't ya?"

The girl said something else.

Charlie just shrugged his shoulders.

"What she say that time?"

"She asked me if I thought in English."

"Do you?"

"It depends on what I'm thinkin' 'bout."

Kuka said: "She ain't got no underwear on. When she crosses her legs, I can see her cunt."

The Latin girl threw her eyes on him quick.

"Hey," Charlie says. He came over to Kuka. "She knows them words." Charlie looked Kuka over. "Say, I'd like to set around with a cup a joe and have a choke with ya, but ... you lookin' for some jack, right? I think I got jus' the thing. Maybe it's a long shot, but ..."

He wrote out a Hyde Park address.

"All you gotta do is get laid," he tells Kuka.

"A private club. No hassles with the cops. Talk to the fellow at the desk. Tell 'im I send ya."

Kuka studied the address.

"Get laid?" he said.

"Yeah. It's fast money."

"This some kind a whorehouse?" Kuka asked.

"Kuka ... you know how Wade's always tellin' you it ain't smart to know too much?"

Kuka regarded him.

"Charlie," he said, "this ain't none a yer shenanigans is it?"

"I got no time for this," Charlie said. "Go down there. Good Lord!" he said. "Look in that far mirror. *Redeye.*"

As Kuka walked out with the address in hand, he happened to glance over at Charlie's desk. On that desk sat one big fat shoe with its tongue sticking out. He could have taken this as a sign, realized he'd been snookered again, but it was lost on him.

Now it has to be interjected here that Charlie Tucker had a bad habit of pulling Kuka's leg. If the truth be known, the reason he liked Kuka a lot was in that he considered him just so damn lame. He watched Kuka leave. There was a bemused expression on Charlie's face.

"You want some lemon drops?" he said to the girl. "Right behind you there. Reach back." And he said in English: "Yeah. They go with yer dress."

Suffice it to say, it was a whorehouse, but of the wrong persuasion.

The desk clerk had a real smoky voice and wore only a tie with a flamingo on it. That's it.

"The po-lice said we *had* to dress," was all he got out before the trouble started. The rest of it is just too absurd to relate here.

By the time Kuka got back to Ybor it was nearly dark, and he wasn't as mad as he'd been. But Charlie was gone anyway, the store locked up. There was a note tacked to the door:

> *Kuka—just a little joke.*
> *Don't be angry. That was not*
> *very nice what you did to the*
> *desk clerk. Here's a number*
> *to call. It's legit. One of*
> *the art instructors at the U.*
> *comes in all the time. They need*
> *models. It's cake.*

(name/number)

*Charlie*

Kuka stuck the note in his pocket. I got a turn this shit around, he said to his mind. Because he knew sometimes, when life turns its backside to you, bad luck and the blues would start to catch fire.

## 15. KELI WYATT

Tuesday afternoon, Kuka hitched a ride downtown. He got let off near the Floridian Hotel. He stood there for a moment looking up to the railing on top of the hotel to see if any buzzards were roosting. Sometimes they'd perch on the railing there and keep an eye on things below—see if anybody dropped a french fry or piece of hot dog. He seen one before with mustard all over its beak. One late afternoon such as this, he'd watched them for hours wheeling in the thermals above the city. This had fascinated him, but didn't sit right—that Tampa had buzzards circling it. The fact he didn't notice any this day he took as a good sign. Then he walked the rest of the way to the university and spoke to Mr. Timrod, Charlie Tucker's acquaintance in the Art Department.

Mr. Timrod was a very nicely dressed older faggot who looked like he also had a drinking problem. He gave Kuka a room number, a time to be there, said the pay was 10 dollars an hour.

So at 4 o'clock Kuka walked into the studio. He had nothing whatsoever on his mind. He had nothing to lose and no idea what he was doing. But as he walked into the room, there was a nude girl up on a raised platform, and he was just taken back.

Because her face was one like on the magazine covers, or a cameo, the enormous mouth, as though her lips were bruised, black hair piled high on top of her head, a long straight nose, and in the pose she held, a total blankness to the eyes—not paying attention exactly, wasn't all the way formed. And her body was full and old-fashioned. Just something caught his attention everywhere he saw.

There were eleven students in a half circle around her drawing on large white pads. Kuka stared badly at the girl for a moment, regained his composure, then looked for a chair.

He took a seat in the back. No one seemed to notice him come in. They did not pay attention to him once he was there.

It was a beautiful room. This part of the university, in the early days of Tampa, had been a luxury hotel. It was a sprawling, red brick Victorian building with wide verandahs and horseshoe arches, and silver minarets on the roof. Set along the wooded riverside, it was exotic and dreamlike. This particular room had a fireplace, and the corner where the model reclined was circular. There were bookcases built into the walls, with old, leather-bound books in them.

He started reading some of the comments penned onto the desk where he was sitting. *Hello, my name is Dick Nose. I'm a hump truck. Welcome to hell, boys. Jackie Jones sucks my bone.* Under that an arrow pointed to—*She's a schitzo. Does that mean she gives head 2 at a time?*

*No, she eats shit twice as fast.*

Mr. Timrod had told him the instructor conducting the class was Ms. Haney. Pretty soon she came back to where he was sitting and introduced herself. They talked a few moments. She reeked of intellect and madness, somewhat along the lines of John the Hat when he was going good, Kuka decided, but otherwise she seemed fairly nice.

"Have you done any modeling before?" she asked.

"Not to speak of," Kuka said.

"Well," she said, "it's nothing to it. There's the dressing booth." She pointed to a little closet. Some joker had painted a star above the entrance.

He said, "What am I to change into?"

"Nothing," she said. "Now get a move on. You're up next."

Well the closet was half full of clothes and books, so he stood a little outside it.

Ms. Haney walked to the head of the class, spoke to the dark-haired model, who suddenly became animated and started twirling her hair nervously with one finger. She stepped off the platform. The first thing she put on was not her robe but a pair of red high heels. It took Kuka's breath away.

Now he already had off his boots, his ballcap, long-sleeve shirt, and he's got his jeans down around his knees when Ms. Haney declares:

"Mr. Kuka will model for us next."

And the entire class turned as one with Kuka standing there just like that feeling about as much like a peckerhead as he ever did in his life.

The teacher made a little joke. "Mr. Kuka, you look good in red," she commented. "Class, the musculature will be more defined...." She went on like that for a time.

So pretty soon he's up on stage, for that's what it felt like, and she put him into a pose that he's not allowed to move from—which gets to be near impossible after awhile. The pose looks like he's about ready to throw a shot-put.

Now Kuka's only brush with athletics occurred once yearly during the pentathlon at the bar. This consisted of pool, darts, bowling, shuffleboard (these last two were table varieties), and fast dancing. So he got those contests on his mind, and inside he started relaxing. Because basically, the students were just drawing. It's not like at the Rag Doll, he concluded, where the audience is out there grunting like farm animals at the strippers.

Then the dark-haired model came back into the room. She was fully dressed and had a drawing pad and charcoal pencil. She sat down and started looking at Kuka and drawing him.

He got to gandering at her, and she saw this and made a little smile. Then she took out a camera. A flash. Once again, no one seemed to notice anything. The shutter clicked. There was a faint whir as the film wound through the next frame. Then damn if she didn't cross her legs, and Kuka caught sight of them red high heels again. Right soon after that, his crank was hard. It rose up like it wanted to have a look around.

"HOLD THAT," Ms. Haney all but screamed. She says, "Yes ... that's good. Class ..." All of a sudden she's writing furiously on the board. Form. Shading. She framed each statement with her hands. On and on. It seemed like to have got her in gear. Out in front of Kuka, one girl tapped another on the shoulder and whispered, "He needs to put a red flag on that."

It was all quite embarrassing for Kuka, but he made it through. It was to be his last known stage appearance.

# 16. CHUTZ

The dark-haired girl came up to him after class and said her name was Keli Wyatt. They stumbled around in a conversation for awhile, then she asked kind of an out of the way question—did he know anything about automobiles? And Kuka said, yes, that he did, he knew how to drive one. So they took a ride in her brand new car.

It'd be nice to say that Kuka and her hit it just right that evening, but after they'd gone to dinner and had a swell time, he took her to the bar. She had one look at Wade, and he looked upon her, and they both of them commenced to get eye lock. And it's far as Kuka got with that.

Maybe at first with Wade it was that he'd found someone finally he liked to fuck just endlessly. They went at it, days and nights of steady-on in which they would only get out of bed to go to work or eat. They stayed naked on Emma Street, wrapping sheets and blankets around themselves when Kuka was there.

She'd go sit with him until he got off work at night, enduring the whores that were constantly fluttering around, the divorcees, the young girls with fake I.D.'s. Or he'd go to school with her, a knife in his boot, unsure of the place, observing it, bemused. And both of them prospered by this and fell in love. Kuka'd never seen the likes of it before—Wade so far in love.

In time their love became something like another person that Kuka grew fond of, but that night he was about alone as he'd ever felt. The two of them had disappeared on him at the bar. Then hardly no one was there that he recognized. The waitress who brought his beer was new. She said her name, but he didn't understand her. It was like that.

Finally, Mickey's girlfriend, Johnnie, showed up. She was pretty loaded. She wanted to shake his hand every couple minutes. She asked if he'd heard from Roy L. before he left. That Roy L. had packed his gear and left town, returned to Palatka to the angel he'd met. That he'd been looking for Kuka all afternoon to say good-bye. Then Johnnie said something else.

"I like your new place," she said. "It's real nice."

This statement seemed to have some weight to it he couldn't quite pick up just then. He had too many things on his mind, not the least of which was the loss of a friend. They talked awhile longer, but then someone came around she was interested in, and she gave Kuka the bum's rush.

He wandered home. The walk did not help him. He stuck around the apartment for an hour or so going insane to the clattering of his thoughts. He began to rant aloud. He spoke at length to the table. He got rough with a lamp. "Why live like this?" He seemed to throw this out to all the furniture present. "It's ain't even livin'!" Whether they, in their detached immobility, responded in any way is not known.

Finally, he stuck the pistol in a pocket of his army jacket and walked up to Nebraska Avenue, then on down toward Ybor City. He stopped on Nebraska at one of those downtown country bars there.

He drank alone for hours.

He got really drunk, and then he drank himself out of that and started to come around to where things made sense again. It was 12:30, and the crowd was thinning out. The barmaid was one of those skinny country women with a boiler around her mid-drift. One of them who was born looking old and had spent her whole life growing into that. She was about as friendly as that kind of odd number is.

There were several groups of yahoos setting at tables and some singles at the bar, and these late-night pilgrims had their bullshit going. You'd hear pieces of conversation:

"So you know who I saw? I saw Vince."

"So?"

"So I saw Vince. I thought you'd like to know is all."

"Fuck Vince."

Or two women who was talking:

"How you like your new boyfriend?"

"He's real fine. I jus' wish he'd stop pushin' on the back my head, though."

Well Kuka listened to this and that, but mostly he was weighing his chances. After awhile, it seemed as if the pistol was jabbing him in the ribs. Like it was egging him on. The only thing he couldn't figure was how, afterwards, he was to get out of there and make his way home.

About then this old man who'd been sitting next to him got up and left, and another one took his place. He was heavy, with a face so flat and round it looked like he talked to you with it pressed up against some glass. He was kind of wall-eyed also, whereby one eye seemed to be looking off someplace else than the other one. Well, it was clear soon enough that he liked to talk. He ordered what he called a barley-pop, turned to Kuka and all but started shouting:

"The world treatin' you all right?" he said.

"No, it ain't," Kuka answered, "but I'm bearin' with it."

Now that wall-eye was on the right side, and he kind of talked out that side of his mouth too, in a wheezing way.

"I tell you," he said. "That's the way I was about it too, say ten years back. Ast me what I was doin' ten years ago."

Kuka said: "What was you doin'?"

"I was in jail," the old man answered.

"Really?" Kuka said.

"It was pretty real. There was niggers on both sides of me."

He'd finished off his beer by then, and he ordered another.

"This'n on the house?" he asked the barmaid, but she deadpanned him.

"Star'll fall from hell 'fore you get a free drink here," she said finally.

As she walked away, he twirled a finger next to his temple.

"Crazy bitch ... say, you ever been here before?"

"No, I ain't."

"Well, see her old man's the one owns this rat trap. And he's crazier'n her. His name's Cowboy Luther, and he's buried out back. He's buried alive out there in this goddamn ten gallon hat tryin' to break the Guinness world record for that sort a thing. See the sign there? They chargin' a buck to go out there an' see 'im, but no one pays a buck, or gives a damn to begin with, far as I can tell. Guinness has professed no interest whatsoever. But he's in a plywood box under the back porch, and he's got a phone in there with him. I mean. My name's Chutz," he ended up and stuck out his hand.

"Now the onliest sane reason I can see he's doin' it for is to get away from that snaggle-tooth bitch. You see how she treats ever'one? She's just too high hat an' always has been. Her family's the damn same. They all peppers. An' you ain't supposed to get in them families 'cept by blood or the ring. But Bill, I mean he married her finally, but mostly he got in by the backdoor.

Kuka bought them both a round. The barmaid said three dollars, but Kuka looked at her, said: "'Bout a few minutes back they 'as only a dollar apiece."

Well she looked at him like, You lucky son of a bitch, how'd you figure that out? Then she took the two bucks. Soon as she left, Chutz started back in on her.

"Look at that hair," he said. "Looks like a cat what's been through some kind a machine." And he added: "Bill was always known not to be too smart, but when he hooked up with her it sorried all of us. 'Bout a year 'fore that occurred, he was goin' to get married to this real fine girl. But he shot the girl he was engaged to's brother. It wasn't never too clear why he done it. There was hand-me-downs about this an' that, but it never came out. Maybe just out a meanness. An' his Mama saved his ass then. She got him off."

"How'd she do that?"

"She sent men with money in their hands."

"What was you in jail for?" Kuka asked him when there was a break in the conversation.

"What it was is that I was doin' some safecrackin' then, an' my partner, who was somewhat a shit for brains, got t'spendin' the money big an' talkin' likewise. We made ten grand that time an' I jus' took my cut an' deposited it to the bank. Well … consequently I checked into Raiford 'cause a this boy's mouth. He did me bad wrong.

"I told the boy, I said, 'Big John, son, you're gonna get our ass in a sling you go actin' wild on this cash.' See, 'cause we wasn't used to gettin' that much. We wasn't even so good at it really. The first job we pull we don't know nothin' 'bout drillin' tumblers. We was usin' glycerin then. We was inside a grocery store, you know, 'bout 4:30 in the morning, an' set it off. Well, we used too much. An' when the thing exploded, the whole fucking safe blew through the wall and landed in the parkin' lot. I shit you not." And he added, "Even then it didn't open.

"But it ain't nothin' I'm proud of. I paid the price, an' it was 'bout a waste a time. An' like I say, it wasn't even my own doin'. 'Cause you don't get the right partner, it's somewhat like pissin' on yer own foot."

One of the ole boys from down the bar come walking by just then on his way out, and he had his fly open.

"Zip that up, Calvin," Chutz told him. "What're you doin', trollin'? You ain't gone catch nothin' lest you get some more bait."

About by then Kuka felt the weapon nudging him again in the side. Because there was exactly two people left in the bar besides themselves and the barmaid. There was one old guy yawning like a moccasin, and a lady in a green cotton dress that hung on her like she had no body underneath to support it. She was staring at her drink as if it had completely stumped her. The barmaid had been hard at it all night too, and she was about on her ass, kind of dicking around with the napkins. She looked like that she hated the napkins.

"I'm gettin' hongry," Chutz said.

"For the most part I only eat in bars. The food ain't so good, but there's a lot of it. Today at lunch I had chicken an' yellow rice, cornbread, green peas, tossed salad, and peaches for dessert and 6, 7 beers. It's somethin' when you look around and see most ever'one else eatin' weighs two, three hundred pounds. Most of 'em have the personality of a rat. They jus' come there to eat. They eat there ever'day and so do you, and that probably adds up somewhere down the line."

"Chutz," Kuka said, "you got a car?"

"Sure."

"Let's go to the Pancake House. I need a ride. I'll buy."

"Might as well," he said.

When they got outside, Kuka told him, just a second, he needed some cigarettes. And he went back in the bar and took care of business. It was a whole lot easier than he thought it'd be. He asked for cigarette change, she opened the register, saw the gun and fainted cold.

# 17. THE WRONG CROWD

Keli wanted to take them to a party up on the north side. It was Monday. Outside the window the day was losing color. Monday nights in Tampa then, a good time came around about every other never. If you went to see your friends, no one would be home. No one at all. It was like as if they'd disappeared. You'd go to the bar—there'd be some diehards setting around, and them trying to ease out of how bad they felt from the weekend.

Kuka said, "These people gone be at the party, they all right?"

"They're jus' so fucking cool," she said. "If you get by that, they ain't bad."

"What's the occasion?"

"I'm not sure. The Chairman of the Art Department's throwin' it. Or his wife rather. It's probably her idea. She's bored or what-have-you. The old man, I can't imagine him havin' fun. He's real dour. He married for money, the story goes … but it turned out she didn't have so much as he thought. He knows that's all a joke now, and it's like when he found out, he wasn't never gonna allow himself to laugh again."

"What's she like?"

"Her nose is out a joint. She don't add nothin' to conversation or to company."

The three of them were sitting at the kitchen table eating olives. Keli had a bottle of Pepsi. Wade wasn't crazy about the idea at all.

"Why you want a bring us along for?" he said.

"So I don't have to go to this shit alone."

Kuka said, "My friend O'Neil, he's an artist. He's the only one I ever knowed … 'fore you."

"What's he do?"

"He makes decoys. He can make a duck, now. He'll take a piece a wood, a block of it, an' start hittin' at that with a hatchet. Then he carves for awhile with his knife. You see a duck start comin' alive under his hand. Then he paints 'em. He's good. Somebody said a couple a those he made flew away."

After awhile he added, "I think his wife said that when she was drunk one night."

He thought for a moment or two, then he said:

"Let's go find Mickey and take him with. They got to deal with him, maybe we can fit in some better."

Wade smiled for about the first time all day.

"That's good," he said. "Yeah … that's a good one."

Mickey was staying with his sister then on a street off Nebraska in a little room she charged him for by the week. They went there. He'd come back from the blood bank not too long before, had money in his pocket, and he was game. He told Keli to stop at Alpine Liquors, and he bought a pint of Old Crow.

Now Mickey wasn't never in too fine a health, but like he was this night, trying to come off Dilaudid, he'd have to stay drunk for some time, and this would cause his stomach to go to hell. Being that he'd given blood and working hard at the pint in the car before they got to the party, his skin sallow and his eyes with that blood/orange color to them, he wasn't a pretty sight at all.

He was just looked like junk. But soon as he threw up, he'd start drinking more, and there wasn't much to say to him that'd make him change.

They were in Keli's car, a little foreign number called a Saab.

"You got a nice room," Keli told Mickey.

Mick just looked at her. He had a pick set, various screwdrivers and pry bars in his room.

"I gotta fart," he says.

"Hold it."

"Anita (this was his sister) fried up some them little sausages. Repeaters," he said. "There gonna be any talent at this party?"

"*Beaucoup*," Wade said.

"I want one with a big rack."

"What's he talkin' about?" Keli said.

Mickey eyed his bottle. It was all but empty.

"There gone be any hard liquor?"

"They'll have things to drink," Keli said.

"What you mean, things?"

"Punch...."

"Maybe I'm overdressed," Mick says. "Look, I need to stop pretty soon an' shake hands with the mayor. Anywhere you can pull over."

Keli whispered to Wade: "What?"

"Where the hell are we?" Wade said. It'd been a pretty good ride. They'd just passed a sign that read Blind Pond Road.

They were hitting 70 down a twisted highway.

"Watch it, Keli," he said. "That guy jus' blinked his lights. There's gone be a cop up here."

But all the rest of the way they watched the roadsides, and it turned out there wasn't no cop.

Well soon as they got there, Mickey headed to the bathroom to check out the medicine cabinet.

"You might ought a keep an eye on Mick now," Wade told Keli. "He's got that disease, what they call it ... where everything sticks to yer hands?"

"Kleptomania?"

"That's it."

Mickey, of course, viewed this entirely different, for he believed all but religiously the junkie logarithm that everything you got really belonged to him, and you were merely holding it for the time being. And he seemed to have come up with some goods because the next time they saw him, about a half hour on, he was spooling out words in a rapid tangle, speaking with his hands, making wisecracks and drawing a laugh from a girl he was talking to, all the time apparently taking inventory of the valuables in the room and commenting to no one in particular what they might bring at the pawnshop. The people around him, meantime, seemed to be trying to figure out if his arms were long enough to get in their pockets. After he got done talking, he juggled his balls several times. The girl looked at him, smiled and walked away.

Mickey said, "Damn ... I tell you. Some nice lookin' trim here." He glanced around. "The rest a these folks, say ... I don't believe we hang out at the same malt shop. Know what I'm sayin'?"

A young girl in a blue leotard and long red shirt, her hair streaked with salt and gold, walked by them just then, and Mickey dropped the conversation and started sidewinding after her.

Now Keli got to talking to this and that person until Kuka and Wade got tired of meeting people. So they left her and drifted outside. There was a large gathering outside, somewhat broken into groups, and the two of them stood at the edges of this trying to fix on what they were into.

Some of the people there obviously weren't used to drinking. There were those who knew something about everything. They talked about movies. They dropped names which everyone seemed to recognize. Some of them just talked about a bunch of shit none of them could make out.

Here, listen to one of them—they found out later from Keli that he was a silk screen artist from Atlanta (this made no sense to them whatsoever)—a slight man with black glasses and his hair slicked down who is dressed rather wildly, though it is obvious his clothes are too young for him:

" ... and there is the added sentiment of going to my hair stylist, whose salon is all in pink and gray, and populated by a certain (he paused here to wink at his audience) clientele ... all of them with a two-minute tan ... now the woman leans over me, but there is nothing to gossip about. Our one sensual moment, the cut where she kept pressing her body into mine ... and yet not any real understanding between us ... except now I tip her, quite handsomely, and now I buy a bottle of this or that hair tonic or cream to lend a severity to my look...." He glanced over his shoulder at this point as if someone had just called his name. After this he cried out, "And that's about enough, too," though it was unclear what subject he was addressing. He finished off by saying, "Alas," then took a handkerchief out of his pocket and honked in it.

Kuka looked at Wade.

"Wha'd he say?"

"It was somethin' 'bout old whores gettin' pumped in the ass."

And they were surrounded by this talk which communicated the sort of intelligence that allows a turkey to drown in the rain.

So they walked around the swimming pool and through the yard. Behind that was a swamp. The moon was shining down through the swamp and onto the red-black water.

They saw Mickey then with three girls. They were passing a smoke around. Mickey was staring at one of the girls. She had on a Clemson T-shirt (she pronounced this *Climpsin*) and a somewhat strange hairdo that looked like she had cut a large wad of gum out of it, but otherwise she resembled a flower, and Mickey all but had her clothes off with his eyes. The girl passed the reef to Mickey. Mick took a sour look at the punch in his cup, said very properly and polite, "Excuse me," turned his head a little to the side and threw up.

Now two of the girls felt a great sadness at this and quickly departed. But that third one had her interest up. To look at Mickey, you wouldn't think he'd have much going for him with the young girls. He was not handsome, though his features added up to something not easily forgotten. He looked somewhat Chinese, with his shaved head and goat beard and earring, but he had that smile, even with the tooth missing, and something about him that you liked but couldn't put your finger on, and he talked confidently to them and made them laugh. They wouldn't look at him at first, but he knew after a few drinks the odds would change, and there was always one hanging around him, usually, like this particular one, with an expression on her face that mixed curiosity and dread.

"C'mere," Mickey said. "There's somethin' y'all got a see."

They followed Mick back inside, until he suddenly stopped and kind of went into a point.

"What is it?" he asked.

Well they studied this creature, and there's some confusion on who said what, but it went something like so:

"She's butch."

"No ... 's a dude."

"Well, he is got tits then."

"What about the mustache, though?"

"She jus' made herself up."

"Wadn't born that way."

"Maybe it's some kind a fashion."

"Must be a gag."

"I hope so," Mickey said. "I had to take any a this serious, it wouldn't be no fun at all."

There was a lady inside who was eighty-three years old. She was a poet. She'd grown up in a place called Storyville, on the edge of the French Quarter in New Orleans, and spent a good part of her life living in Paris, France. She had a delicate, genteel Southern voice and manner that charmed you as she spoke. And she was pretty quick. When Mickey left the room once, she said, "Does he think sideways?" Well that folded them up there. Wade was the only one who didn't laugh.

She talked about Paris in the 20's and 30's, of the artists she was friends with, and the times it'd been. She talked about a man named DuChamp. She was still in love with him, though he'd been dead some many years. Her hair was white as milk. Her eyes were lavender. She was rail-thin, and her face just almost a skull. But there was something about her, something beyond her appearance—how she took in the world, the way she moved in her chair—so that her beauty was gone and yet somehow undiminished.

"What was you thinkin'," Kuka asked Wade later on, "when we talked to the old lady?"

He looked at Kuka kind of funny. "Well," he said, "to tell you the truth, I was thinkin' about fuckin' her." He said, "Man, that Paris, France ... that sounds like a place now, don't it?"

They walked back outside, carrying on and laughing. Now when they got out there, some music was playing real loud, and Mickey said something to the effect:

"The hell is that? Sounds like a bunch a damn coon tunes."

He says that and walks on, but here comes this guy up to him, kind of fat and jowly, who somewhat resembles a frog. This association was brought to mind or perhaps just accentuated in that he wore a dark green suit.

Kuka took one look at him and immediately thought of what that ole girl had told him once when she learned of a brief romance Kuka'd had with an acquaintance of hers. "When you get home," she said, "you'd better check that frog a yers for spots," is how she'd put it.

This fellow says to Mickey, "Look ... say, look here." He seemed to be quite agitated. "Your reference to coon music wasn't well received here," he said.

Mickey looked around, then looked back to the man and said: "Where?"

"By myself." He poked himself in the chest with his thumb.

"The generic reference of description you used ... while being colorful, perhaps, and colloquial ... just carries too much pain for many folks I hold dear."

"Who're you?" Mick said.

"Dr. Hartwig," he said.

Now the unexpectedness of his remarks caught Mickey at a disadvantage, but that didn't last long. Mick disliked doctors in general and grouped them all in one category—quacks. He stole a glance or two off to the left. Then his head swung back around, and he studied this guy as if only then aware that he existed. And he just studied him square in the eye, sizing the man up as he was want to do.

"Well?" the man said, and he looked at Mick and nodded as though he expected some answer. Then he set his jaw. But Mickey, a kind of smile took his face, and he looked the man over some more as if trying to see what he was like inside, and in the meantime, didn't say nothing.

You could see the man get anxious about then. It's possible he had obtained a clear view into Mickey's eyes. Because whatever Mick'd taken from the medicine cabinet had him pretty well baked. He couldn't even blink. And you seen already the man knew he'd shouldered too much and wouldn't mind to get out from under it. Perhaps he was over-tired, the evening had become a bit strained, he might call it quits early.

"Funny how language can load up like that," he said. But just by looking around he could tell right off none of them knew what that meant. And his spirit faded then, and what remained seemed like that which disappeared, but it really wasn't the same.

Mickey cocked his head, closed one eye, and spoke finally:

"You from out a town, ain't chu?"

The man's shoulders sagged under this.

"Say," Mickey said to him. "Since you come this far, take another step, motherfucker ... an' see what you take back."

Well Wade stepped in then and put an end to it. For the past minute or so he'd been both bemused and slightly horrified at the thought that this might be one of Keli's professors, or even the Chairman himself.

"You don't want a do this," he told Mickey. "Let it ride." And he got his head bowed, his eyes aimed low.

It was all the man needed. He jumped. He all but disappeared in mid-air, but now Wade and Mickey were squared away with their ears pinned back.

Then Mick backed off. He took his girl by the hand and walked, said over his shoulder, "I was jus' gone have some goddamn fun, Wade."

Soon after this, Wade and Keli hooked back up, and Kuka started wandering around alone. He walked out back to the swamp. There was smoke coming off the water, and he remembered that O'Neil called this "witch's hair."

He had four conversations out there of note.

Kuka had on a ballcap with a Browning sticker on it, and this kind of dumpy woman came up to him and asked:

"Is that Browning, the poet?"

"Ma'am?"

"There on your hat … is that Robert Browning, the poet?"

"No ma'am. I don't guess so," Kuka said. "I suspect that's Browning, the gun."

Secondly, he spoke briefly to O'Neil, who popped into his mind all of a sudden, over vast distances and far out of earshot, but they talked nonetheless.

*I don't know what to say to these people*, he told O'Neil.

O'Neil answered him, *You jus' got a learn to fall right.*

Other than that piece of mysterious advice, it was just a conversation Kuka had in his mind, but it was good to have a friend there, even for a moment, that he could speak to naturally.

Then later, he ran into Mickey. Mick was at the edge of the swamp. He was on the ground and flopping around like something that'd been shot. Kuka went over to him and helped him up.

"My leg grabbed on me," Mick said.

Kuka said to him, "Man, you look like shit."

"I don't know what them things was I took," Mickey said, "but they had a hell of a detour to 'em."

"Where's Johnnie tonight?" Kuka asked. He was just making conversation.

"Who knows," Mick said. "Ever'time I see her anymore, she's got the blackass. Got the molly-grubbers. She's a pain in the ass."

"Fuck her then," Kuka said.

"Yeah," he said. "Well, somebody is, I know that."

"What you mean?"

"You know damn well what I'm sayin'." And he stalked away.

Kuka didn't understand it at all.

Finally he began to wander up to small groups of people. He'd stand around, listening to what they said but afraid to speak himself lest it got stuck in the conversation. More often than not, they would sense his presence and drift away. He'd go over to another batch, and he might hear like so: "They may not have rewarded me with my leather easy chair yet, my friend, and perhaps a little while longer before I have enough credit to order a glass of port…." And he did this until he came to the conclusion that they were all just chewing cud.

But at one group—there were three couples and a few strays—his mulish nature surfaced, and a contrariness came into play. When they tried to walk away from him, he would, governed by a perverse stubbornness, lock right in step behind them. Maybe it was just that they acted like he wasn't even there, talking away like they didn't see him amongst them. They were discussing the various stages of the moon, and Kuka threw into the conversation a quote of O'Neil's (Kuka himself had never understood the concept, but he said it anyways):

"Don't never set a fence post durin' new moon," he commented. That turned some heads.

Another one of them said how they'd been down in the Glades and fishing off a dock and how this Great Blue heron stood around there, and they'd fed it pin fish.

Kuka said, "Them big birds? 'Bout yea high ..." He held his hand up to his chest. "They're partial to hot dogs," he said. "They'll eat a hot dog."

Nothing. They ignored him totally.

Then another one started saying about the need for bulk in their diets. Someone else mentioned greens. A little while later, when the conversation had almost shifted, Kuka said somewhat lamely, "I like olives...."

## 18. NELL JORDAN

There is a certain bedevilment in the darkness of October. Kuka growled at it. His voice rose in testimony against all the months of the year. He cursed a skink that got underfoot, mocked the frogs for their croaking. (There were no frogs croaking. It was but that the swamp coughed—and a nasty cough it was.) He cut his eyes back to the party, the shape of light there, thought of the electrical street corners where prostitutes argue. "All a them are dogs," he raged, "turnin' themselves into hoops to bite their tails."

This broke along the swamp. Whippoorwill, hoot owl, they had something to add, and the swamp hens clattered in the pickerel weed. Then the path accelerated and twisted into the night, and the horseshoe moon crashed down and made the swamp a slatey blue. So that finally, when he had lost his breath, he was deep in this blue.

Now the trail continued on alone—staggering drunkenly into the dark. He stopped by two maples that braided around each other. He just lit a cigarette and leaned against the sky, the star-blaze, the enormous dark. Red leaves started spilling like wine. He bent down and studied himself in a puddle of water. In the moonlight he was almost handsome. Only when he looked closely in that face could he see the things life had done to it.

He put his hands to his temples, grimaced in the tannic water; there was something wouldn't be shed. Something for him alone that the wind must not pass along, or the forest with its many sayings. Like the soft ruffle of cards in a game of chance, the swamp wheezed in the cattails, and the cypress ran all about.

Now had it been spring, the answer would have found its way into this sooner. But it was autumn, when the mind begins to reflect on the fall of the heart rather than its rise. So when the girl came toward him, it seemed like she came walking out of his own wild thoughts. She disappeared in a curve of the trail, then stepped apart from the night, clarifying in the wells of the moon—a front tooth framed in gold, stars on her long hair.

"You been livin' here all your life?" she asked, and her smile was full of play.

"Not yet," Kuka said.

"I'm a friend of Keli's," she said. "We're best friends. She was minded to leave you out here for bein' so mean to them people...."

Now Kuka, as this girl rambled on, recalled one night at the bar when Wade'd said something surprising.

"There's some girl keeps askin' 'bout you," he said.

"Who?"

"I don't know her name. A friend of Keli's."

"Asked what?"

"What's yer girlfriend like. That kind a shit."

"How's she know me?"

"How do I know? All I'm sayin' is, she's been askin'." Then he stopped and thought a moment. "She saw a picture of you or somethin'," he added.

"Good," Kuka had replied. "I hope she comes around. I'll have at her in the manner and fashion of our brother the dog." He was a little drunk at the time.

"You friends with them otherns?" Kuka said now.

"They're all right," she said.

Kuka said: "They jus' so in the know. They talk like books. They must read shit all the time. Me, I got word blindness. I don't like to even say too much. I don't want a give myself away."

"They smart in other ways than you are. That's all."

"They rubbed me wrong," he said.

"Did you really call them varmints? I mean to their face?"

"I can't picture myself sayin' that. It must a been some other body."

Everything about her was dark, until she laughed now in the moonlight, when her eyes turned green like they were new.

"I didn't get yer name," Kuka said.

"Ravenell," she said.

"You got a boyfriend?"

"Kind of," she said. "But I'm 'bout to give him the ax. Come on," she said. "Come with me. Let's walk down to the river dock. There's a fairy tale about this swamp. I'll tell it to you."

And she put her hands against his chest and stood on her tiptoes—because she really was kind of little.

"Will you come home with me tonight?" she asked.

"Well, I guess," Kuka said.

Then for a long time she told him quite a story, though she spoke no more words.

## 19. GREEN ORANGES

He woke the next morning under a quilt in a bedroom he didn't recognize. Everything around him looked antique, like that he had woke up in the past. An old, Stevens sawed-off twelve gauge leaned in the corner. The wallpaper was faded and had yellowed and made pastel the fields of wildflowers blooming there. There was a night stand with a drawer. There were daguerreotypes setting on it. He studied the faces of the people in them. They looked stern. He opened the drawer and found a loaded .38 snubnose. His clothes were folded on a rocking chair, his boots on the wood floor. He wrapped the quilt around his waist and got up to check his wallet.

Ravenell came into the room then in a light yellow sundress, barefoot, her hair in braids. She smiled at him, and her smile had that mischief in it. He remarked to himself how very pretty she was—a doll face, something almost Oriental to it, her little girl breasts, her womanly ass.

He stared at her. He hadn't noticed in the night that her hair was streaked with gray.

"What you lookin' at so?"

"Yer hair," he said. "I've heard tell it's a sign of meanness for a young girl to have gray in her hair."

"It's true," she said, and smiled some more—the gap between her two front teeth, the one framed in gold.

"You needn't count that," she said. "There's close to a thousand dollars even. You al'ays carry so much cash money?"

He didn't answer her. He said, "How'd we get here?"

"My truck. You was pretty much trashed by the time we left."

"I guess I ought a get dressed," he said.

"If you like." She smiled again and went away.

"You want some coffee?" she called back to him.

"I'll take a beer."

"I'd have to go get some a that."

"Get a paper, too."

"Hey," he heard her say. "You kind a tellin' me more'n I want a hear now ... you workin' it, ain't you."

She came back into the bedroom with black coffee and a piece of lemon meringue pie.

He looked out the side windows. There was a dirt lane and pasture on the other side of it with black cattle grazing and egrets at their noses, and what looked to be ten thousand spider webs spun along the ground, each one caught up in dew. Out the back windows there was an orange grove, the leaves a deep, waxed green, and the oranges still green on the trees. A Carolina wren sang somewhere near, and everything was enclosed by the morning fog.

"Where are we?"

"You're in Turkey Creek, Florida ... come on, put them britches on. I want a show you my place. An' I ain't gathered the eggs yet, jus' so's you could help me."

Kuka smiled. She was like a little girl kind of the way she said that.

"Yer boyfriend ain't gone come 'round here is he? I might want a be doin' somethin' useful if he does ... say like cleanin' some these guns."

"He's out of the picture," she said.

Her house had wood floors and ceilings, braid rugs thrown here and there, the whole thing grown inward from the walls, all of it a little dusty, and a cool wind coming in that made the curtains breathe. An easel stood in the dining room and paint tubes scattered around and brushes in coffee cans. She had one of her own paintings on the wall there—made of lilies and ibis and Indian corn—that was beautiful and all color and energy. A kitchen sink stacked with dirty dishes, wooden-handled knives and cast-iron pots and pans hooked to the walls, a little basket of red tomatoes and another of bananas on the table, and the smell of bananas gone ripe. A fisherman's creel hung on the wall also, full of purple berries, and an old print that was a picture of Jesus in a storm.

"What're these?" Kuka asked of the berries, for his eye was drawn to their color, and he'd seen them before in the woods when he was young.

"Callicarpa," she said. "They jus' somethin' grows wild, but they're pretty. Mama calls them 'Beauty Berries.'"

There was a Franklin stove in the living room with kindling and fat lightard stacked beside it.

"That stove don't draw so good," she commented. "When it's cold out, it'll take the edge off this room. That's about it. It don't come near the bedroom."

When they sat down in the living room, there were mirrors they sat down in too, and through the screen door, the wind spoke in.

Later, he couldn't recall too good what they said to each other. They laughed often, and would look at each other and look again. It was a little frame house with a tin roof. It was painted white with dark green shutters, surrounded on two sides by grove. She said that her Granny owned it all. There were old live oaks in the front yard with long beards, a row of mailboxes in the corner where the dirt lane turned. Across the main road there were strawberry fields.

She showed him the azalea bushes that surrounded the house, told him the colors their flowers would make. She showed him what she called wine-and-milk lilies that some kittens were playing in, and more kittens in the bed of her '51 Chevy truck, and a mama cat doing figure eight's through her legs.

She had a chicken coop with Rhode Island Reds looking through the wire, the hens turning their heads to one side then the other, blinking as if they were deep in thought.

They gathered brown eggs in a wooden bucket. There was another live oak in the backyard with a picnic table under it. They played horseshoes. She wore a bonnet. The autumn sun burned his face. Then it was cool under the oak, drinking tea with lemon seeds floating in the ice and eating bread-and-butter pickles that she placed before him on a piece of waxed paper.

In time she checked the mailbox and no mail. Showed him her garden gone to weed, and only tomatoes left, long overgrown their stakes and leaning heavily upon themselves. Two squirrels made a fast bracelet on the limbs of the oak tree. The sweet smell of cow manure in the air, the field across the lane now auburn, oat, butter. And the day went away like that, marked by the simplest things.

The wind moved the fields and the leaves on the trees and the hawks above, as the prettiest girl showed him that what she loved.

She was a little country girl with all her stories about the past, and she loved to tell them, and everything, as she spoke, was kind of lazy and many years ago.

They went inside finally, and it took them some time to get to it— at first she kept looking away from him, like she were ashamed or afraid. But she got laid down anyway on the bed, over close to him and smelled his hair. He made her dress so it didn't cover her, and she had nothing on underneath. And the clover and sweat of her, and the not looking one more time as she rolled over on her belly.

He took her from the back the first time. He took her that way, and then he took her from the front, and called to the voice that slept in her body.

She gave herself away and smiled into the pillow. She gave herself away so recklessly.

They stayed in bed and made each other sore. They stayed all tangled up for three days and nights.

They made love everywhere.

# 20. THE DIARY OF A LUCKY MAN

Then the phone rang. The world and what it meant had not touched them. They were in another place, away from all that. And it rang some more. It was a black phone that hung on the wall in the kitchen. They were eating bacon and eggs. They stared at the telephone like as if to answer might be to get snakebit. She picked it up finally, said hello, put her hand over the mouthpiece and said, "It's Keli."

She cradled the phone on her shoulder as she lit a cigarette. Leaned against the wall and took a draw. There was a long silence before she responded. She said, "No shit?" She fretted with the cord. "Ain't no tellin'," she said. "How come, you reckon?" Then handed him the phone.

Keli said to him: "The cops come here lookin' for you."

"Where you callin' from?"

"A pay phone," Keli said.

"Okay, look ... was they wantin' Wade, too?"

"No," she said. "He was here. They asked him for identification. They didn't say nothin' else to him. They had a warrant. But they didn't say why they wanted you. There was three of 'em. The one was cool, an' the other two were nervous wrecks. They was runnin' all over the apartment with their revolvers."

"Keli ... I want you to get my clothes. Put them in my duffel bag ... the pistol's under the mattress."

"I'll put the duffel bag in the back seat of my car. When Wade goes to work tonight ... you know what I'm sayin'?"

"Thanks," he said. "I won't be able to go in the bar...."

"No. Don't."

"So tell Wade I said take care. An' you too, Keli."

"What's it all about?"

"I ain't sure. It's nothin' to do with y'all."

"Be careful. We'll send you money if you need it."

She hung up.

Ravenell had gone outside. He pulled the curtain to the side and looked out the window. She was underneath the oak tree picking up something. When she came back in, she had a handful of green acorns. She opened her hand and showed them to him. Then she started crying and turned away.

"Damn it," she said. "I jus' hate to bawl."

Kuka started to say something, but he stopped after a couple words.

"What?" she said.

"I forget."

"If you forget what you was gonna say, Mama claims it was probably a lie anyway ... come on ... what's the lowdown here. Keli said the cops come around."

So he just told her. Told her this and that because he wasn't sure all together himself and was trying to add it up as he spoke. But there wasn't any rhyme to it.

"Far as hittin' that bar, I didn't tell nobody. I didn't even say nothin' to Wade." And he added, "I don't know what to do."

"You got to git," she said. "Ain't no way 'round that."

She was pouting. "No," she said after awhile. "No, they cain't take you 'way from me. I jus' got you."

Kuka started thinking out loud: "I need a ride to the bar tonight. So's to get my gear. I got to get hold of O'Neil...."

"I know a place we can go," she said. "I'm gonna pack. Mama's got some land up to North Carolina. I'll call her. She'll come see after the chickens. Come help me will you ... help me get my suitcase down."

"You might get in trouble you do that."

"I don't care, Shug. We'll jus' go there. It'll give you time to think anyways. Shoot ... I'm havin' too much fun let you walk. Let's go there ... do some things we never have. I'll call my brother right now and get some reef lined up ... maybe some 'caine. Look, this ain't the only damn place to live. I'll make a list ... come on ... we have to function a bit more smartly now."

By dawn the next morning they were past Atlanta heading north on 441. They had lived all night on coffee, done some lines, talked about things they couldn't begin to remember—all the wherefores and etc.'s of it—stopped once to eat at a truck stop, not hungry but needing something, once to make love in the cold autumn air in the yellow leaves outside an anonymous town that was sleeping, their breath like white scarves flaring from their mouths.

Then the day opened to the painted trees, smoke rising off pumpkins, silos, church steeple, orchard—light and shadow spangling the truck window. They went down through Asheville, south to Bear Wallow Mountain, down into Hickory Nut Gorge to Bat Cave and the Esmeralda Inn.

They slept.

Kuka dreamed he was a lucky man, that he was known for this, that he'd been famous in love, that money was easy.

"If I fall for you," he told her late that afternoon when they awoke, "you're not gone fuck over me now are you? 'Cause I seen what it does to people. That it makes 'em different. They fall in love with a person, but that changes ... an' they're still in love with the old person, but she ain't there no more. I don't want a end up haunted by love such as that."

She'd just done some of the 'caine, did too much for just getting up, and in a moment she said, "I want to have two babies. I'll have a little girl for me an' a boy for you. I'll spoil my girl-baby, but the boy is got to be raised hard an' sharp."

They were lying in bed, he on his back and she with her head on his shoulder. Kuka rolled his eyes.

He commented to himself, Kids drive me nuts. Kids an' dogs, I don't like neither one. But he added, Though I've met some nice dogs the last couple years.

"Will you marry me?" she said. "We can get married an' have a chivaree."

He said: "Look, that old man at the desk told me they serve dinner out on the porch. Let's go see what they got. I'm gettin' hungry."

"No," she said. "I ain't doin' nothin' till you promise. An' we gone seal the promise in blood."

She took the knife from his boot and touched the blade to her little pussy that was all swollen from their fucking....

That evening she ate a golden trout that was so big it hung over the plate.

# 21. RED VELVET CAKE

Next morning the air was sharp and had a faint yellowness to it like clarified butter. A wind would come up sometimes and tug at your clothes. Or the trees would suddenly become full of energy, and leaves would fall, or four-and-twenty blackbirds might spill down the sky. Along the gorge the stream rang against the stones. Then the wind might stop as quickly as it began, and the sun would get kind of lazy on your shoulders, a sense of smoke in the air. And tomorrow and yesterday fell away also, and thoughts flowed of their own accord without overlay. They went down to Lake Lure for breakfast, and the people at the restaurant were calling it an Indian summer.

"As opposed to last year," their waitress was saying. "That was the rattiest autumn I've seen. It was jus' rained steady on then. An' the fall rusted out. But this year's been cool and sweet, an' ain't had that killin' frost."

She was a bit long in the tooth, with honey-brown hair and a kind smile.

"Now it says in the paper it's gone rain this afternoon. But I don't believe them weathermen anymore at all. They all look like they need a drink, you ever notice? It comes down to them talkin' 'bout the day before, I might believe 'em. Otherwise, forget it."

"Well, it sure is nice an' warm in here," Ravenell said to her. "Our room last night in the lodge, now that was jus' too cold. It'd be a good place to hang meat."

Kuka had begun to notice that wherever they went, Ravenell had that smile about her, and people took to her right off and spoke. They soon learned her name and called her Nell or Honey. It was wild for him to understand.

"Randy Lee! Randy Lee!" the cook called out from the kitchen.

"Virgil," their waitress said, "I know my name. I been usin' it all my life."

So Ravenell got to laughing at that.

"Hey. That's a good one. Where'd you get that from?"

"Oh, I make up things like that all the time. It jus' goes through my head an' comes out my mouth."

When they paid their bill, Randy Lee said:

"You folks ought a come back tonight for supper. I'm gone make my Red Velvet Cake. It's famous here abouts." She looked around, then lowered her voice. "Confidentially," she said, "it's damn near a sin."

Walking under the maples along the root-broken sidewalk to the truck afterwards, past the windows of the restaurant, the people inside smoking, and talking with their hands, Ravenell said to him:

"That sausage was slightly gamy," she said. "But now them biscuits an' brown gravy—Shug, I thought I'd died an' gone to heaven ...."

She was looking up the road.

"I can't believe this," she said, "but I still have an appetite. Wadn't there a place up there's got soft ice cream?"

"Maybe we should come back for some a that cake tonight," he said.

"You ever had any that?"

"No, I ain't."

"It's a pretty cake," she said, "but the icin's made out a lard."

She said, "You know ..." and she reached back and slapped herself on the ass.

Then all of a sudden, there he was kissing her and feeling her up in broad daylight on Main Street.

## 22. THE DAYS STACKING UP TOWARD WINTER

The camp looked unused for some time, but that once great care had been taken with it. It was laid out on three terraced levels. They were connected by stone paths that stepped down before you. It was in a hollow that water from the spring above had made over all the years. The spring turned into a little creek that ran alongside the camp, but it wasn't much—at some places a single leaf could change its direction—and you had to wonder about the patience and long strength it took to cut the rocks there and to smooth them.

The top level was the largest. They set up the tent there. The second held the fireplace, a circle of stones. The third was a narrow ledge where you could sit and hang your legs over and look down to the valley below.

On the first day, when the light was at its warmest, butterflies rolled in the air, dark ones hatched out of time. They fluttered around like the bow ties of referees. There were little yellow birds with black masks and a nice song—"Mama always called them wild canaries," she told him—and between them and the creek, bits and pieces of the day were discussed into the dark.

They would sleep late, waiting for the sun to start the morning. They had sleeping bags of eiderdown she'd gotten from her brother. Kuka would get out of his reluctantly. Or he might wake sometimes to the smell of coffee and bacon. He'd sit on a big flat rock by the fire in a flannel shirt, his Army jacket, a quilt around his shoulders, and eat bacon and bread she'd fried in a skillet, drink coffee from a tin cup. After awhile the sun would angle down the poplars and maples, and it and the smoke from the fire would make blue stripes through the camp.

Every other day they would go down the mountain for supplies. It was a twenty-minute drive down a twisted road like a roller coaster to a little store off Garren Creek. Then back the long way through a valley of farm land, the leaves red and yellow on the hills, tobacco curing in the barns. Only the cabbage fields were green here, the clouds gliding gently sideways above them. Then the turnoff onto the dirt road of the mountain, a winding cut, steep in the hillside with blackberry hugging its edges, up one last almost vertical climb where it leveled off and curved toward the spring.

The spring ran out from under a huge, mottled-white rock, and there was a sense to it that this was the heart of the mountain. They would park the truck there and take a drink with their hands. Rhododendron followed the water over the hill and down to the camp below. There was a feeling of timelessness to the spring. You knew Indians had drunk here, and countless generations of animals, and that maybe

God too had quenched His thirst on its wild sweetness.

When he kissed her below the white rock, the spring would grumble like an old grandma.

And though the camp was pitched down from there maybe only a hundred feet below, it was invisible from the road. Of the time they spent there, only one car traveled the road. It went up the mountain, then back down. They did not catch sight of this, but only heard it.

In the afternoons they would work around the camp, adding stones to the walls that held each level, flat stones to the paths, gather firewood for the night. Just the going up and down so much changed things.

Sometimes they'd walk the old logging roads that crossed the mountain. Rabbits liked these roads also, and pheasants ran them. They found a deserted orchard on the other side, good yellow apples on the trees, that what the coons and deer hadn't gotten to. At night after supper they would follow the road above the camp, sit on a log and watch the sunset. One evening, the clouds took the shape of a red fox with a long, bushy tail. The tail must have stretched into Tennessee. She said of this, "It's the dreams of light." Though he'd sat back up straight some time before, when she said it, she could still feel his mouth on her nipples. It'd be like that—he couldn't stay away from her very long.

You'd see lights come on then from houses in the mountains you couldn't tell were there in the daytime. Or maybe a lantern blinking along an invisible road. Then back to the camp, staring into the fire and embers and watching the sparks fly off. And in the dark in the tent they'd get all tangled up again.

At night around the fire, they'd tell each other things maybe they shouldn't have. One night she wanted to know what it was like in Nam.

"What was it like? It was the end of your childhood," he said.

"But some good come of it. The friends you made. It's where I met Wade. At a place called The Rockpile. He was with the 101st. His outfit was laid over at The Rockpile for awhile. An' he had some shit on him, you know—opium. An' we got to be friends. That'd happen quick like that sometimes.

"Everybody was always comin' an' goin'. Somebody's DEROS'n every month. You'd never see nobody for more'n six months, say. People'd get hit, or rotate out, or go to another outfit, you'd never see 'em again. Never know what happened to 'em at all. It was almost like they'd set it up that way—like they didn't want you to find yer people. It's been 10, 12 years. I ain't never run into one a them boys again, 'cept Wade. One day I seen his picture in the *Tribune*, that he's got a fight in town.

"But he had this great shit, an' we went in a bunker, an' fired up. It was amazing—he would take more shots, bigger shots than anybody. He's drawin' back three cc's ... you know, they had it all bottled up even. We had already bottled shit, little tiny milk bottle lookin' thing, like a big, farmer's five gallon milk bucket and had a little rubber stopper just stuck in the top, then a piece of plastic was laid over it, and a rubber band tied around the neck. I mean it wasn't no five gallon can. It was just a little tiny thing 'bout the size of yer thumb—they'd go for ten bucks a pop, an' you'd get a couple shots out of it anyhow. But he's doin' three cc's, an' run it right up the line. An' I do like one cc, one and a half, an' I'm fucked up." Kuka started laughing. "I'm fucking gone. An' we walkin' around the camp later, he's tellin' me, you know, 'Hey, straighten up, man. Notice what yer doin'.'

"I remember askin' him that night, 'Wade, what you gonna do when you get back?' An' he said he didn't know. He said, 'I don't even think I'm goin' back.'

"See, the gook, he's an industrious little fucker. It was industrious for them to make a lot of money off this particular drug that grew wild there all the time anyhow, an' see if they couldn't kill as many Americans as they could with it. But you there, you don't give a shit. You'd do anything jus' get through it.

"But he come back. To Ft. Bragg. He had maybe a year left to do. Ten months. And he couldn't make it. They didn't like his attitude. He got busted for possession. They didn't catch it on him, but they knew what he was up to. So they bust him down to Private-E-Nothin'. Like that tour in hell don't mean a thing. Didn't mean a thing to 'em. An' he did a hundred days in the stockade there. In the Army they can keep you a hundred days pre-trial. So he told them jus' let him out, which they did. But he was in the can a hundred days anyway, till this happened—till they drummed him out.

"An' they still fuckin' with him about that. He goes to the VA to get somethin' done, they still askin' about that, you know—Where was the heroin? How'd you ditch it?"

"When was you there?"

"1968 ... I come in-country in February. February 9th. You never forget that date, see ... 'cause a year later you leave the same date. It's what you livin' for. Yer goal in life."

He said, "I think I run into Wade sometime 'round Christmas that year, 1st of the year, maybe, in '69. He'd jus' been there since November, but I was gettin' short."

"Keli loves him so much," she said, "but she thinks he's crazy ... it don't matter to her that he is, understand...."

Kuka smiled. "He ain't like other people. Ain't nothin' half-way with him. He's still out on point. He's got these home-made laws he lives by. One a them is you don't show yer hand, like I'm doin' with you now."

She kissed him. "It's okay, baby," she said.

"Yeah, but see ... he lives by 'em. It's all an eye-for-an-eye with him, all that old Bible stuff. He's the wrong person to get on the bad side of. 'Cause you do that, yer fucked.

"But I got back, an' I went to California for awhile. You could get 104 dollars a week unemployment there. That was much as people was makin' then workin' their ass off for it. So consequently, there's a bunch a vets there ... an' we all jus' pretty much stayed fucked up all the time.

"That's when I started takin' acid. This orange-barrel, four-way hit. Incredible. This is down in L.A., which is probably travelin' about the speed of light then. But to me, after Nam, everything is very slow. L.A. in slow-motion. So I start takin' acid, an' I do this for a hundred days. Until I get strychnine poisoning. Which all but kills me.

"So I come back to Florida. For R&R, see. Try to get my head screwed back on. But it's like Wade does a hundred days in the can at Ft. Bragg, an' I'm kind a doin' the same ... only I put in a hundred days in the ozone.

"But I come back, like I say ... an' I was jus' had totally lost track of Wade or anybody else from there. An' it's '74, '75, till I seen his picture in the paper, an' that he's fighting that night at the Armory in Tampa. An' I went an' saw him. I couldn't fucking believe it. An' nothin' hadn't changed. It was like that we hadn't seen each other for a weekend or somethin'. It was good to see a friend from over there. It really was. It made all the difference in the world. 'Cause the people I was hanging around then was jus' bullshit.

"After he'd got out, he went home to Minneapolis, an' jus' dicked around—same as I'd done. For years, you know. Doin' drugs, foolin' around four, five years. It's hard to get started in the world . You ain't in gear at all. Spend most yer time tryin' *not* to work. Tryin' *not* to get a job.

"But he'd started his prizefighting. An' when we hooked up again, he jus' moved down to Tampa, 'cause the fight game was hot there. Always has been, off an' on. An' I started goin' with him on the road. Minneapolis a lot, Arizona, New Mexico. We went up to Cincinnati, places like that. Sometimes he'd get fights along the way from one place to the next. They'd call up the next town, say, you know, we got a tough guy comin' yer way. An' he's still doin' his shit. Almost up till the end of the prizefightin', he's still doin' it. That was his biggest fight then. He couldn't shake it. It was jus' one them times, where it was makin' him sick, an' the only thing keepin' him goin', too."

"How you do that," she said, "an' still fight?"

"You take a light shot," he said. "An' some them fights he was in, get hit like he did, 'cause he got his eye fucked up, see, but he kept fightin' anyways. The eye works, but the depth perception's off—the thing you need, right? He had an operation. He even fought a couple times after that. No dice. He kept gettin' hit with the right hand he couldn't see comin'—that he couldn't judge the distance of anyhow. But he had 15 fights or so like that, with one eye.

"But like I say, to get hit like that, he probably should lisp now, or blink too much. All them towns with tough reputations ... the house-fighters, them what got the blue chair in their corner, they'as some hardass motherfuckers, now. An' the refs wouldn't cut Wade no slack ... but he made it out okay, jus', you look at him close, some scar-tissue draws back his eyes a little...."

"When you went along with him on the road like that," she said, "wha'd you do?"

"Not much. Mostly jus' I was along for someone so he could talk to. My only real job was I'd go make bets out in the house. You knew he wasn't gonna get beat. I mean he did sometimes, but mostly it was a sure thing. An' we made some money on that angle.

"Then a couple years back, he jus' gave it up. That string ran out, an' he got the job at the bar. He always knew he'd get a job like that, see, 'cause one time he dreamed he was the bouncer at The Last Supper.

"But it'd took him almost till then to kick. So we started sellin' shit, but least he wasn't takin' it no more. It wasn't easy for him to do that. Not at all. An' it was jus' strength of will what did it finally.

"But like from the time I run into him again, I'm settin' on top the world. To me it's like I'm someone else, an' that person I was before ... I mean he was a mess, you wouldn't a cared for him. He jus' never found his itch in life, you know what I mean? But from that time, like I say, till now, it's like I'm makin' myself up from scratch as I go along...."

Soon after this, she went into the tent to get some smokes. The tent was dome-shaped and light tan in color. At night with a lantern on in there, from the outside it called to mind a luminous egg. When she returned to the fire, he started talking again. He couldn't shut up. He talked himself backward in life:

"One time ... I was still livin' at home ... my old man called me a shithead. He said it out loud like that—'Hey, shithead.'

"All his life he's got one hobby an' one job, an' they both was that he drove a truck. It was all he ever fucking did. Runnin' fertilizer to Miama. Limerock from Brooksville to Tampa. I used to go with him sometimes when I was little—otherwise you'd never see him. You'd never see him when the sun was shining. If it was dark, then you'd see him—in the morning or at night. I'd go with him in the summers, when school was out. It'd be 120 degrees in the cab. The tires might be meltin' by two o'clock. An' he loved it, an' I never could figure it.

"If Mama was workin'—he'd talk about her job in these terms, you know—'My wife makes the equivalent of about a half a tire a week.'

"*Shithead* ... an' he didn't cuss, see. Never. It shocked hell out a me. Mama was there, over to the side of the kitchen. She was cuttin' lettuce or somethin'. She wouldn't look at me. The cops'd been around. My family didn't want a have nothin' to do with it. I can't blame 'em really."

"What happened?"

"I'd back-talked an officer of the law," he said. "John D. Law, you know. But see, I'd grown up with this asshole. I mean he was older'n me, but I knew who he was. 'Fore he got to be a po-lice he was into petty theft. Holdin' up people with a comb in his pocket ... this sort a shit. An' we traded hands. It wasn't nothin', but he made a big deal out of it.

"But it was jus' topped it all off. I was s'posed to be in the 11th grade then, but I'd dropped out. I couldn't hold a job. Them jobs I had, it'd take 'bout two days, if that, to figure 'em out. To figure out what you was doin', an' by then you'd already started to hate it. Same with school. They'd give you them tests, jus' so as to make you look like a fool. I know how to read an' shit. I never learned numbers too good. Nothin' ever added up right. The answer never turned out like they said it was."

Kuka laughed at this for some reason.

"It was a small town. Inverness ... you ever been there? This is 'fore it started growin' like hell. I was related to 'bout everyone in town. Even my kin then, they'd tell me—'Yeah, come around.' But when I'd go see them, they wasn't so glad that I'd did.

"After that it was like—get drunk all the time an' fight yer oldest an' dearest friends. Anything for entertainment.

"An' it seemed whatever I tried, I was gettin' dealt into this shit I didn't know how to play. Jus' everything seemed to backfire on me. I was jus' this hick from a little town. I parted my hair on the side. Even when something went right, I'd have a hard time accepting it. It'd be like, say when you was little an' some kid gave you candy—it was probably 'cause he didn't like that kind, right? So I got a choice to go to jail or into the Army. I don't know if they even do that anymore. I hope they do."

"You know," she said, "over there, you said it wasn't so bad ...."

"I don't remember sayin' that."

"You ever talk about it?"

He said, "Maybe to another vet. Otherwise, it ain't nothin' I want a keep on my mind."

"Wha'd you do there?"

"I was a grunt."

"Was you at where they was shootin' an' all?"

"I was up along the Z," he said.

These last two answers hadn't meant a lot to her, but she kept on.

"I don't mean to act like I'm prying," she said.

"I jus' don't know if you'd understand is all."

"You didn't have to kill nobody did you?"

"That's what I mean," he said.

He lit a cigarette.

"It's somethin' in me," she said, "to be curious. I remember when I was little, comin' up here with my folks. Lookin' in people's houses at night. Makin' up lives for them."

Kuka didn't hear her so much. He was staring into the past, thinking on some friends of his.

"Honey, you said you was there in '68?"

"Yeah."

She ran that through her mind.

"It's been 14 years."

"That don't matter," he said. "Don't matter how long it's been. It ain't over yet."

Then he said, "I say their names sometimes. When I'm goin' to sleep ... whenever it comes up ... on Memorial Day ... I say them. Like Alfredo. Everyone called him Lit'l Bit. Didn't nobody use their true names up there much."

"What happened to him?"

"Lead poisoning," he said. "We was on this firebase. Jus' the tiniest piece of shrapnel." He put a finger to his forehead above the right eye. "All kind a shit flyin', an' he caught this one little piece with his name on it. He wasn't but 18. He was just a kid. We all were.

"A Tex/Mex from down there somewheres. He was teachin' me Spanish. But I don't remember any of it now. Eighteen—an' Ole Scratch come upon him. But see, like now, he's a long-held friend. All a them. An' what you say 'bout that place, you say for them, too.

"It's like you been showin' me how things are here in the woods. That the livin' an' the dead stand together."

He called them in then—"Yox, Smoky Joe, Lodi, Sully, Maniac, Cooch...."

# 23. JO-PYE WEED

That Thursday the Indian summer broke, and it started getting downright cold. They rented a cottage at Lake Lure. They left the tent and most of their gear at the mountain. It felt good to be clean and warm again at night, to make love in a bed all but seemed luxurious, but otherwise there was something not nearly the same. Down in Hickory Nut Gorge—in Bat Cave and Chimney Rock and Lake Lure—all anyone talked about was closing up shop for the winter.

Friday they went into Asheville to the flea market. Afterwards they spent half the day looking for a bar. They found out there weren't any. That was the telling factor far as Kuka was concerned. That pretty much sewed it up.

"We need to go someplace where it's civilized," he concluded.

They decided to go back up on the mountain and stay there as long as they could take it. Then leave.

Sunday night, two hound dogs got loose from down below somewheres and ran rabbits on the mountain. All night they brayed in the dark. It seemed to change everything, as if this had created atmospheric mischief.

In the morning the sky frowned. Dark clouds gathered and started blinking. An angry storm roamed the mountain. It spun around the mountain, wouldn't get off it. The wind started howling. The trees creaked. It brought to mind the songs of whales—seals barked—a little baby cried. Lightning broke everything to pieces, and the sky just spilled down. They'd peek out the tent every once in awhile. The forest looked like it was being shook by the back of the neck. Then bolts of lightning started exploding around them like ordnance.

Inside the tent, Ravenell was braiding her hair.

"Do you want a live at my house?"

"I don't know," he said. "Maybe we ought a go someplace else ... I know I can't handle this much longer."

"I mean," she said. "If I die today, I hope I go to hell. Let me put it this way—it might be the onliest place I'll ever be warm again."

"We stay at the house," he said, "I'd get careless."

"Let's see ... I could get my brother, Donny, an' Mary Lou to come live there. I have three thousand dollars in the bank. I got more really, but ..." She would say one thing and braid her hair, and after awhile say another. "I can get my hands on that. I jus' don't want a live in the city, though. Mama always told me I wouldn't be happy with a city man. Honey," she said, "can we go have Thanksgivin' with Mama?"

"Oh, Lord," he said.

"It won't kill you. She's nice. I know she's dyin' to meet you. An' you ain't even know my brother yet. I love him."

She finished braiding her hair.

"How do I look?"

"Baby," he said, "you're a beauty ... an' you know it, too."

"I don't," she said. "I'm not nearly pretty as you." When she'd say something like that, she'd nod her head yes for awhile.

"You jus' gone blind is all. I ain't been pretty since I don't know when." Then he said, "I remember though ... when I was yer age ... yeah, all them girls wantin' t'give me their number ...."

She kissed him.

"You're disgustin'," she said. "Shug ... I want you to promise me somethin'."

"Say what."

"If somethin' bad happens, jus' somethin' ends up wrong betwixt us ...."

"Ain't nothin' gonna happen like that," he said. "We're too lucky."

"Let's jus' say, for the sake of argument ...."

"I don't want a hear it."

"You jus' never know. You might drop me over somethin' I ain't got nothin' to do with ... but anyways, if somethin' does happen ... let me finish ... let's meet here in the spring, an' be together again. Okay? We'll come here an' make a stand."

She kissed him once more.

"It's beautiful here then. The trillium bloom, an' the lady's slipper. An' the dogwood. By May the whole mountain's white with dogwood ... the hickory nut trees. They have a purple flower like wisteria. The wild strawberries flower, an' the raspberries, an' the fruit starts.

"Used to, there was an old trough under the spring that collected water. I'd like to get another one. You could touch the sky in it, catch clouds in your hands.

"Later on the little tree frogs start up. Thousands of them. They sing at twilight, jus' a few of them at first. They sound like goats then ... or old car horns—a Model T or somethin'. But by dark, it's a giant handsaw cuttin' through the forest, the back and forthness of it.

"The wild iris an' thistle and jo-pye bloom...." She held up her hand as if she had something in it. "See, if you hold a jo-pye in front of your mouth, what you talkin' 'bout will come out in your favor ... will you promise?"

She kissed him a third time.

She said, "It's jus' a shade embarrassin' how I want you all the time so...."

Outside, the storm raged on. They made love in a dancing house. Next morning, a cloud had settled on the mountain. The last leaves were down, the camp blanketed by them. They walked a strange land then, amid objects made of crystal and glass.

They crossed over the mountain to the wild orchard one more time. As they returned, she said to him:

"Maybe someday, when we're very old, we'll enter that dreamy, cloudy place we go to when we're alone ... an' we'll simply forget the steps that lead back."

Then in the afternoon they broke camp.

At the bottom of the hill, an orange school bus stopped and spilled its last kids, then pulled away with a grinding sound. There was a house trailer at the bottom of the mountain, machine parts scattered in the yard, a shed made of clapboard, a Ford Mustang up on blocks. There was a red Doberman chained in the yard to an old front-loading washing machine that was its doghouse. There was a man holding a ball peen hammer. Two tow-headed kids set down their schoolbooks and started choking a baseball bat. The dog barked. The man put a quid in his mouth, and as every time they'd passed, he waved. Then they were down the road, and the scene was erased.

They didn't look back. But it was one of those times so good it left a mark on you. And in return, part of you never left.

# 24. TOOTSIE WASHBURN &
# LITTLE CATHERINE MARSAGLIA

They got back home around noon the next day and fell asleep. But Kuka, by that night, was want to roll. The two of them had been together solid for some time, and he just felt like seeing the big town. He was restless. When he felt that way, he would do things that made little sense, even to him. He took the truck and went to Tampa. He called the bar to leave a message for Wade. The voice on the other end got quieted.

"You got a name?" it said finally.

"Yeah."

"This you?"

"Sparky?"

"Yeah."

"Hey," Kuka said. "What's goin' on?"

"A bunch a shit. I ain't so sure 'bout this phone."

"Let me talk to Wade."

"He ain't here. He's up to St. Paul. One his brothers got in some trouble. That's what he said anyway. I didn't get the particulars of it."

"How's Keli?"

"She's around. But I don't know where. They got bogged down 'bout somethin', the two of 'em. Ever'thing ain't coincided between 'em of late." She put her hand over the phone then and said something he couldn't hear. She came back on. "Deuce says to tell you, Hey. Look," she said, "there's too many new faces in here. I don't know what it's all about. I don't know where they all accumulated from. You understand what I'm sayin'?"

So Kuka went up to Tootsie Washburn's. He lived north of town, up near the beginning of The Road to Nowhere. Toots was about Kuka's height, but he weighed 300, 320, somewhere in there. His chest looked like a shelf. He was a debt collector for a guy named Santo Ragano. You would see this name in the newspapers from time to time. They called him Santa Rags.

If Toots wasn't working, he kept a low profile. He could be found at home much of the time, listening to the TV at wrestling or what have you, for he didn't like to go outside so much. He'd stay home, which he kept cold enough that you had to dress for it. Kuka knocked. He notices Toots has a new door. He heard Toots working the locks.

"Hey," he says. "How you been do? Come in. You're in luck. I jus' got my prescription."

Now it's freezing inside the apartment, but Toots' bald head is sweating like mad. And something is wrong with his left arm. It swung around like a scarf whenever he moved. Toots explained it: "This redbone hit me with a tire iron. I don't know what he thought he was dealin' with. Maybe he didn't know he was in a gunfight. That boy was a disgrace to niggers all over. But say, it was completely dead from the shoulder on down. I'm startin' to get some feeling come back into it. I think it's gone be okay."

Kuka said, "Toots, I need some shit. Jus' to put me even, you understand."

"No problem," he said. "Set down. You gotta try this what I got. I gone take an' cut some this out. You hungry, best eat right now. There's some Braunschweiger. Eat a cracker. Otherwise, fuck it. You ain't gone be hungry pretty soon anyways.

"I made a run this week. Up to New Jersey. Them dudes up there, they nuts. Dark glasses at midnight, zoot suits, the works. Shit like that, I don't know. Down here, they'd stand out. I ain't used t'workin' with Guineas. My clientele's strictly Cuban and Bloods. There I'm dealin' with two guys named Buster Indelicato and Stogie Joe LaBrussa. Great big ole wide-headed cats. Got muscles in their heads ain't never been used. They like two butts passin' in the night. Scary fuckers...."

On TV, Gordon Solie of Florida Championship Wrestling was describing the finer points of what sounded like "a high vertical soufflé."

"Oh my goodness!" Solie said. "He'll feel that in 20 years. I'm not lyin'...."

Toots brought out an 8-ball and put some cut down on a mirror. He set some off to the side and made a line about five inches long and hit it. Then he contemplated the TV for awhile.

"That was Katherine's share," he said, speaking of his wife.

"What's she up to?"

"Her an' Little Catherine's out to the bars."

"Little Catherine?"

"Yeah ... here, try this ... cut it in half. You do that whole line all at once, your brain'll solidify an' fall off yer neck. An' Little Catherine comes back here, she's bird-doggin' now, she'd fuck any somebody, but I'm tellin' you there's some talk she's got the heebie-jeebies. So you get to her by some mistake say ... don't tell me I didn't warn ya."

Then he and Toots spoke nonstop for two, three hours. Later Kuka don't remember much of what was said. They covered pretty much the all and whatever of it. The conversation ended up like so:

Kuka: What happened to yer door?

Toots: I broke it all to fuck. A couple weeks ago....
My legs kept swelling up. An' I'm angry all the time.
That part took care a the door. So I went to the
doctor. The doc puts me through some tests. Couple

hundred bucks worth. So I go, 'What is it, Doc…
what's wrong with my legs?' An' he says, 'Yer havin'
trouble with yer legs 'cause a bein' overweight.' An'
I say, 'So how come I'm so irritable?' An' he goes,
'That's because yer an asshole.' So basically, it costs
me two bills to find out I'm a fat asshole … which
is pretty much common knowledge to begin with. But
what about you … what you been tryin' to say? I
don't get it.

Kuka: That I fell in love, I guess.

Toots: No doubt. (He rolled his eyes.)

Kuka: With this little Alabama girl. That's where her
family's from anyway.

Toots: It's the worst kind … them Alabamer girls'll love
you tooth an' nail. Is she got any dough?

Kuka: Maybe. I don't know. She's about the prettiest
thing I ever got mixed up with.

Toots: What's that got to do with anything?

Kuka: She's got the prettiest little mouse on her. I can't
see what she likes about me, though.

Toots: It must be on account you was reincarnated from a
goddamn mule is why. Them Alabamer girls can
spot a mule.

Kuka: Reincarnated? I don't much believe in all that.

Toots: Well, far as I can tell, ever'body's for it, an'
ever'body else is against it. But it's somethin' you
might ought a start to thinkin' on. You keep on like
you're doin', you ain't gone last long. This backdoor
life a yers'll soon lead to ruin.

Kuka: I can't believe you say that. Look at yer hand …
you can't even hold a beer without shakin'.

Toots: I didn't have the shakes or an occasional coughing
spell, I wouldn't get no exercise at all.

Kuka: An' you jus' admit to me awhile back you killed a
man last week.

Toots: (Laughing) I fast-drawed him … but I didn't say I
killed him. I jus' lightened his load some.

Kuka: Only exercise I get is fucking. My cock's in the
pink, I'll say that. But now I gotta meet her family
come Thursday. I can't picture 'em takin' to me.

Toots: Hey, they don't like you, fuck 'em in the ass. If
they like that, fuck 'em in the nose.

Kuka: This thing with her … I'm jus' gone break it off.

Toots: (Toots blinked at him.)

Kuka: Jus' end it.

Toots: What for?

Kuka: 'Cause I like her too much ... way too much.

Toots: See, right there, that's what I been sayin'. You're a
goddamn mule.

Kuka: I don't know. I jus' ain't got much to say on that.

Toots: We ain't sayin' nothin' here, Kuka. We jus'
talkin'.

Well they peaked at what seemed like about a hundred words a minute, and it was 3 a.m. Kuka didn't know if he should do another line, or if in fact he'd already done way too much. He was in that state of confusion. He was feeling somewhat removed. Then Toots' wife came home with Little Catherine Marsaglia in tow, who is referred to that way, though she is by no means small in any respect. And it comes out that Little Catherine has a boyfriend she's nuts about, but he went home to Ohio for a week, which, far as she's concerned, her thinking right now is—fuck that asshole. And see they were drunk to the point that Little Catherine had fallen down once already and stubbed her nose.

She sat next to Kuka on the floor, leaning against the couch. They knew each other from the old days, which is about three years ago when she was eighteen. And she commenced to let her skirt drift up. Now with Kuka there was always these girls coming at him with some more goods, who knows why, but her knees were skinned up from the fall, and since the last time he'd seen her, she'd gotten braces on her teeth. It wasn't like that she was a kid anymore, but there was some of that to it, and something metallic and predatory about her mouth, so that what happened was pretty soon his rig got hard, and she just put her hand over it to keep the thing around.

Toots and Katherine did a double-take on this, and then they were gone to bed.

"You still hangin' around at the Cadillac Bar?" she asked.

"Pretty much," Kuka said. "I ain't been lately, though."

"Last time I'm there," she said, "some guy's out on the dance floor in a wheelchair, you know ... dancin' with some chick, an' the lead singer in the band had a crutch. Depressed the hell out a me. An' there's a guy in there ... I notice him 'cause he keeps starin' at me all night. He's got 'bout the flattest face I've ever seen, an' I ask somebody after awhile, 'Who is that asshole down at the end of the bar?' Asked the bartender I think. An' he says, 'He worked over at Cypress Gardens for a long time. He's the clown that used to ski on his face.'"

All the time she's talking, she's playing with Kuka. Then she took out his equipment and placed her fingers kind of deep in her mouth, pulled up her skirt, put some spit on her leg up against him and began to work him around on it.

"I could tell you a story. What kind a stories you like?"
She put her hand in her mouth again.

"Dirty stories," Kuka said.

"Uh-oh," she said. "Well ... imagine that I'm with two women. One with dark hair an' one's blonde. An' both of 'em have long breasts, an' their nipples are gone shaded a deep red with lipstick. An' say (she put her hand way in her mouth) ... oh, one of them jus' put her tit in my mouth ... an' say their pussy's hair was all wet ... now they'd made me sit doggy fashion on a bed ... they'd tied me up, an' started to hit me on the ass with a rope, one of 'em did, an' the other one stuck her head underneath me, an' dragged her tongue down my belly ...."

By this time Kuka was humping her leg like a dog, and really, he'd lost track of the story. But she had hold of her own self then too, her eyes almost closed, mouth wide open in a look of deranged ecstasy— then came in a long, cat-like moaning which ended up in a shriek to where the neighbors probably sat bolt upright in their beds, and you could hear Toots in the other room cursing.

Afterwards, she started back on Kuka saying, "Now ... if you can imagine ... you really are a dog, no ... a wolf. You're a wolf ...." And her hand sucking on him. And he came around finally, she milked him dry, and just held it there in her hand. Then they talked a little, an odd conversation in which they seemed to pretend nothing had just happened, and she still held it there in her hand. Did she want to save it? Kuka wondered.

He'd had her before, a few times, those some years back, but she was a strange one even then. She was the only girl Kuka ever knew who would get horny after she ate. Food set it off. And it worked every time. So in the old days he'd always be calling her up, saying, you know—"Hey Cat, you hungry? Let's go get a bite to eat."

It was just a secret of hers that maybe she didn't even know. And he'd come upon it by accident, and was grateful for the knowledge, because otherwise, in those days anyway, she was kind of hard to get to. She was sort of cold. And he's thinking about this when here she goes into the kitchen and opens the icebox....

# 25. THANKSGIVING

He didn't get home until dawn, and Ravenell refused to speak to him. Sure, she said a couple things. "There's bad faith somewheres," and also, "You been startin' to go wrong on me." Neither did Kuka talk. For awhile he was sick with hangover and withdrawal. When he got over that, his feelings were gone. He felt nothing. Nothing could touch him. Nothing at all.

Then it was Thanksgiving. They went to her Mama's for dinner. She lived in Tampa, not too far away from the bar, down by Tampa Catholic High. Ravenell's granny was there, and her brother and his girlfriend, Mary Lou. Kuka took to Donny right off. He wore his hair long in a ponytail. He had a hangover and looked to be in total misery, but yet he kept his sense of humor about him.

He confided to Kuka, "I'd have to feel a hundred per cent better in order to lay down an' die. On the way over here," he added, "it didn't feel like I was drivin'."

Granny was in her eighties, and though some of her remarks seemed to miss the point and her stories to come to no conclusion but would end when she put her fork back in her mouth, she was otherwise pretty spry and surely never at a loss for words. Apparently she was famous among her kin for wandering into sentences she could not find her way out of.

All Kuka knew about Ravenell's father was in that once, during a night at the land, she mentioned that he'd took sick and died. She hadn't remembered the date exactly, other than it was that January day in 1977, when it snowed in Tampa.

Mary Lou looked to be Latin, but she told Kuka that she was part Cherokee and the rest pure Cracker. She could talk your leg off too, and Ravenell's mother was the same. Pretty soon over the meal one would raise her voice to be heard and another would raise hers, and then they were all shouting. It was all good-natured, only a bit loud. Kuka just smiled and ate. He ate way too much, perhaps out of nervousness, and then Mrs. Jordan finished up the meal with a cheesecake that pinned him to the chair.

"My stool don't look right this mornin'," Granny started it. "It was green. Ain't s'posed to be green," she said.

"What you mean your stool ... you mean your shit?" Donny said.

"Yeah, my stool. You got a brown, you got black. But green?" She crossed herself.

"Was it soft?" Mrs. Jordan put in.

"No. It's a little balls like rabbits ...."

She rubbed one hand with the other.

"My asteritis is damn near killin' me," she went on. "My vitabraes is all mushed." She glanced around. "Scuse my English ...."

Ravenell looked at Kuka and smiled. It was the first emotion either one of them had shown for awhile, and he closed his eyes. But her smile was still there, and he climbed into it, after awhile, like a little boat and laid down and rocked against the voices of the conversation.

That night, back at the place, Keli called. She'd found out from Sparky they were home, and later on she drove out. She had changed some. She'd dropped some weight and was even more beautiful than before, but she was dolled up as a two-hundred dollar whore, a long slit up the side of her dress like a gypsy. She had a habit of sticking her finger in her hair and twirling it, and that night she was just twirling the hell out of it and was depressed.

"Wade ain't comin' back," she said. "I jus' know it."

"Why you say that?" Kuka asked.

"Jus' because," she said. "All this weird shit goin' on. We stayed in a motel for awhile after you all left. The cops had kept comin' around looking for you. He started living by the window. Watchin' for the prowl cars, he called them. I tell you ... after awhile, I don't even know if they was real. I saw one cruise by. He wasn't even lookin' our way. He was eating a fucking pizza or somethin'. They was comin' in the parking lot at the bar, hasslin' ever'body. It was drivin' him nuts. An' the other day he hears Cecil's out a jail, but ain't nobody seen him. An' then he's up an' leaves." She talked different now. She talked tough in slang.

"Last night I did somethin' really stupid. I went up to the Rag Doll an' danced. I didn't have no money left. So I went there an' danced. It was horrible. An' they made me fill out a W2 form, so they got my address. I didn't even think to give them a wrong one. I know damn well they don't pay no taxes. Look ...."

She took out a big, crumpled wad of bills from her purse. It was some serious cash there.

"Perverts," she said. "I ain't even counted it. God, I feel sick."

"How is yer dancin'?" Kuka said.

She looked at him. She laughed a little.

"It don't favor anything," she said. Then by her looks you could tell she was running something through her mind.

"You know 'fore I hooked up with you an' Wade, I'd totally lost it. I was goin' to church about every four hours. I went to an AA meeting. I don't even drink. I wanted to hear some stories that was worse'n mine. I'd go to the little picture booth in the mall—get my picture taken to make sure I was still existed ... stop that, Kuka, you're makin' me laugh. It's harsh to survive at jus' goin' to church," she added.

"You goin' back to the Rag Doll?"

"Hell no. I got fired. Toward the end of the evenin' I slapped one a them sex addicts upside the ear.

"You know ... I never could hold a damn regular job. One summer when I was in high school I got a position at the mall. It was one a them doughnut places. You had to wear a stupid uniform, the whole bit. I got fired the first day. But I'm too embarrassed to tell my Dad. So every morning for a week he takes me to work, then picks me up at 5:30. I'd spend the whole day walking around the mall in this uniform. Can you fucking believe it?

"Look," she said, "before I forget ... Wade told me to tell you ..."

"Say," Kuka interrupted her, "you got his number? The Minnesota number?"

"Yeah," she said.

"Sparky says one his brothers got in some trouble."

"God," Keli said, "she can't get *anything* straight. He had a fight ... you know, what is it? Golden Gloves.

"I called him this morning. I told him. Told him 'bout the Rag Doll."

"What'd he say about that?"

"He's pissed."

Well Kuka had to smile some. Because he knew Wade had a jealous streak to him. She had his number all right. Kuka found out much later that he'd come back to town the very next day, but Kuka himself was out of the picture by then. That night he called O'Neil. They talked for some time.

After Keli'd left, he and Ravenell sat around kind of speechless. They sat opposite each other in the living room. It was uncomfortable. Kuka said finally:

"I don't want you mixed up in this no more."

"You're not stayin' on, are you," she said.

"No ma'am," he answered.

# 26. DEPARTURE

Rail thin, scowling, armed with a shillelagh and guarded by pitbulls, O'Neil came to the house to pick up Kuka. It was late afternoon. The sky was fat with rain. All the cats around panicked and dove underneath the house. When she saw O'Neil, Ravenell went outside and started throwing mash to her chickens. She did not say good-bye, nor look their way again. She stood with her back turned to them among her hens.

"What you got that club for?" Kuka said .

"I ain't never sure what I'm gettin' into with you."

"Let's go quickly."

"You breakin' hearts again, boy?"

O'Neil took the old back way, Route 92, into Tampa.

"Why you goin' this road?" Kuka asked.

"There's somebody needs to talk with you."

"Who's that?"

"Hazel."

"Where's she at?"

"Elton Slater's bar," O'Neil said. "She's workin' today."

"So what's it about?"

"It's to do with Madonna Smith," O'Neil said.

On the way to Elton Slater's, the sky got all tangled up into a storm. The two friends rode without talking.

The sign on the bar said "Slater's Sporting Goods & Tavern." You could buy a rod and reel there, shotgun shells, live bait, church keys, a Hav-A-Hank and so on. Toward the back of the store, past the ammo, is a bar with seven stools and four tables and a jukebox. It was dark and stale, and outside there were only lonesome roads and rundown shacks upon which the rain fell.

O'Neil sold his decoys to Elton Slater. Elton was a book-reading man, bespectacled, shy with the spoken word. A short, round-faced man with a crew cut. He always kept his left hand in his pocket—it had the palsy in it. He never seemed at all comfortable with people, and did not give any visual impressions whatsoever of being interested in his business. Far as anyone knew, he'd never taken a drink in his life. As a barkeep he was somewhat hard to get used to. He and O'Neil had grown up together in Valrico. What he did have was the sense to hire good barmaids, and Hazel Swank was one of these. She'd worked this bar since anyone could remember, and sometimes she filled in at The Cadillac.

Elton Slater spoke to Kuka: "Hazel's over by the juke." So saying, he placed the two mallard decoys O'Neil'd brought on the sturdy wood of the bar and began studying them.

Hazel was sitting at a table with some pipe fitters Kuka recognized from The Cadillac. There was an empty chair beside her, but when he went walking toward her, he saw her put her hand down on it, so he didn't stop. He said hello and passed by and sat some tables down. The jukebox was playing a slow country song, and several couples were shuffling around.

There were large mounted bass hanging on the wall over Kuka's head. They had plugs in their mouths. The fish had turned black from years of bar smoke. He sipped his beer and thought—I jus' want a get into the mix a things a little. But it was like he was explaining it to Nell Jordan, talking to her then as he had not at the house. I know that you, he continued, that you've aimed to please me in every way ... but sometimes that gets harder the more you try .... He was talking to her like that in his mind.

Finally Hazel came over. They were old friends.

"Can I sit here?" she asked.

"I don't know," Kuka said. "Do you bite?"

Hazel looked like a skinny old whore, in a black wig or either it was dyed—it was too black to be real. She was sharp-faced, kind of hardened looking. Her age would have been hard to guess. But she had such a pure heart and good sense of humor and liveliness to her, Kuka'd always felt attracted to her.

Her husband was a pipe fitter. He spent most of his time on the road. Kuka'd only seen them together once. He was an old biker, huge and mean-tempered. Every once in awhile Hazel would show up in town with a black eye.

"I'm sorry I couldn't talk right at first," she said, "but this is got to be private."

"What's up?"

"Well ... you know I'm friends with Madonna."

"Yeah. So what?"

"There's some information she wants passed along."

"Let's hear it, Hazel."

"First of all, she don't understand why Wade's angry with her."

"He ain't angry with her," Kuka said. "He's forgotten her."

"That's what I figured. Secondly," she said, "she says to tell you Cecil ain't the one tipped the cops on Wade."

"How's she know that?"

"Cecil told her. He's been hanging around with her some."

Kuka took a bite of that and chewed on it awhile.

"It makes sense," he said finally. "He knows that's one place Wade won't be comin' by. But say ... she ought a get Cecil off the line. He ain't no good. I don't know how far I'd go believin' what he says either."

"Hey," Hazel said. "Myself. He's the sorriest thing since the invention of bullshit. But I'll tell you, none a this don't mean jackshit to me, one way or t'other, 'cept in that it's about made a mess out a Madonna. She ain't got over Wade. Not by a long shot. That sent her for a loop. I don't know what he's got goin' for him. I suspect it's (she held her hands about a ruler's length apart), but damn … he's 'bout all she thinks on."

"So why's she dealin' with Cecil?"

"I got no idea in hell what that's all about. I can't get no grip on that. But she says to tell you this, an' that it's a true fact—Cecil ain't the one what talked."

"Yeah, well, that's his version," Kuka said.

"It jus' don't add up, man … they didn't pop him for nothin' big. He was in the stockade for 30 days. It sounds like pocket-money crime to me."

"Maybe it wasn't longer 'cause a them names he dropped."

"Look at it this way—who put the finger on Cecil? How'd the word get out?"

"Best I remember," Kuka said, "it was one them off-duty cops comes in the bar."

"But who told you that?"

"Mickey did."

"There you go," Hazel said. She said this with a sense of finality.

Kuka just looked at her. It seemed to all but put him in a trance. "I don't see it. Turn it over for me," he said at last.

"Well, far as I know, a cop's a cop, whether they off-duty or what. Why'd they be givin' information to Mickey for?"

"Maybe he jus' overheard it. I don't know. I jus' can't picture Mickey doin' something like that 'gainst Wade."

Hazel shook her head and looked at Kuka like maybe it wasn't the smartest thing she'd ever heard said.

## 27. EMMETT PIKE MOVES AWAY

The next Wednesday, when Wade came to work, he started carrying some cases of liquor out from the back room. This cowboy walked up to him. He'd been drinking long enough. He was pretty fired up and just felt like talking some.

"Tell me," he said. "What's the difference between these two?"

Wade looked at the cases. There were two cases stacked up. There was a case of Jim Beam and a case of Old Crow.

"Well," Wade said, "the difference is, this one is on the top, an' this one is on the bottom. Gone," he said. "Get out the way."

Approximately about the same time, some twenty blocks down the road, Deuce turned his big Oldsmobile into the parking lot of Jilly's Tavern. There was a substantial line of cars behind him, and they was glad to see him get off the street. Deuce'd buy a car based pretty much on the condition the payments was 25 a week and that the electric windows worked. He might say purchase a car what's transmission was shot full of sawdust, but this was a matter of no concern to him. Consequently the windows would go up and down real good, but top speed on the thing'd be 20/25 miles an hour, and whenever you rode around with him, he'd have a string of cars behind him at any given time. He could pretty much tie up one section of town.

Well when he turned into Jillys, he was already a little drunk. He was trying to walk natural, but what he was doing was high-stepping it. Jillys is one of those nice bars that no one goes to, where maybe on Friday afternoons they would serve, like the places before his time, cheese, and say poorman's drumsticks on a platter set out on the bar, and they wouldn't charge you nothing for this.

Most of the bars Deuce frequented had certain things in common— the beer was cold, you could spit on the floor, they got pool tables, and all of them was dives. But earlier that day he had fenced some color TVs. He had made a hundred bucks and hadn't done nothing but act as a go-between. He hadn't been too sure about one of the parties, however, so he'd gone over to borrow Wade Bonner's pistol. "Whatever you do," Wade had told him, "don't fire the fucking thing." But there had been no trouble. So he had some greenery in his pocket, cash flow, and he walked into Jillys feeling good.

He looked around. It's a classier joint than he's used to, that's for sure. There's a couple cornballs around in polyester and clip-on ties. Some other dudes playing the pinball machine. Deuce struts up to the bar and immediately hits his crazy bone on it. No matter. He lays down a hundred dollar bill in the coin of the realm.

"You want a beer?" the bartender says.

"I try not to drink without one," Deuce says.

The bartender wasn't amused so much. He commented to himself, "This guy thinks he's the meaning of life."

Deuce gets his change and makes sure the quarters are dry. His hands got the misery in them, and he's convinced it is caused from years of picking up wet bar change.

"Thanks. Here," Deuce says and hands over a tip to the bartender.

Well at the same time he does this, he just involuntarily cuts one, and cuts it loud. Deuce looks around, looks here and there and says:

"Damn, who cut *that* rose?"

Then lo and behold, this one man with his back turned looks around at Deuce's voice, and there he is—Cecil's standing there big as day.

Deuce's beer stops half way to his mouth. He sets the mug down, then picks it up, draws off about the whole thing. Cecil's giving him that broken smile of his.

"Hey, Deuce, aintcha gonna speak? C'mon."

"Up yer ass," Deuce says.

"Well I'll be go to hell," Cecil says.

"For you it'd be a short trip."

"Whatsa matter you?"

"You dropped a dime on Wade. Everybody knows it."

"No," Cecil says, "you wrong. All a yas."

"Like I say, shove it harelip...."

Then Cecil threw him out the bar. He tagged him once with a cheap shot and just picked him up bodily, Deuce wasn't a very big guy, and threw him. When he did this, his jacket pulled up and the bartender saw that he is packing.

"Get the capgun out a here," he says. "Get yer own self out, too."

"Fuck you," Cecil says. "Who ast you for opinions."

"Keep the sumbitch covered then," the bartender says. Because really, he isn't making enough jack to be dealing with this.

"Be polite," he says, but Cecil's already forgotten him. Then the door's busting open and Deuce coming in, Wade's pistol out in front of him leveling. And before Cecil could draw his own gun, a noise goes SHEBANG! and the gun mangling, so it looked for all the world like Deuce's hand exploded, the shrapnel squealing backward to his heart.

And suddenly Deuce's legs are dancing in that wrong attitude, as he twirled in a sublime and circular way inward to the astonished moment of his death.

A while later, when the big cop that covers the beat come in, he put his finger to Deuce's neck and says as follows:

"You don't need a ambulance for this one. Jus' get a bag."

Emmett Pike, he in the dark place. He don't answer. Emmett

Pike has moved away.

That morning, in the hour when even the streetlights appear to be dreaming, Wade heard it all from Reba, one of the waitresses at the Waffle House.

"Wade," Reba said, "it's one those things that you hate to do it, but there's somethin' I gotta tell you."

And she told him the story as it had come to her through the grapevine.

"No," Wade said.

"It's a fact."

"Who knows it?"

"Everybody an' his brother." And Reba added, "I feel jus' terrible. If I had a dog, I'd go home an' take it out on 'im."

Now the second man involved had skipped before the cops come, but Wade recognized the description all too well.

"Knowin' Deuce," Reba said, "I bet he died happy."

"I bet he don't remember," Wade said.

"He was a dude," Reba went on. "Some kina cool thing. Always wearin' them sunglasses. He'd wear them sunglasses indoors ... an' ever'one knows the sun don't shine on the inside."

"Tell me about it," Wade answered.

## 28. DEAD-EYE JACK

Somebody had given Wade a ride. He didn't know who, or did he even understand it until the taillights pulled away, and he turned around to see that he was home. There was Keli framed by the light of a window, her long black pretty hair tied up in a ponytail, as if she'd known somehow the night would be a long one. He felt nothing. It was like that he didn't even know her.

He walked on through the night, the dark cold and beautiful, into the city of the thin, oblong face with the dark skin that shone when the street lights touched it. And his thoughts and the boulevard was got all tangled up, as he walked past the cops and the sailors and the daughters of the sidewalks, who saw him and turned away, for he would stare at them with an expression odd as the look of the horses on a merry-go-round. So that they might be heard to comment to themselves or to one another, "You ever get the idea that all of a sudden we're on the wrong side a town?"

A dog barked. A tough car gunned down the avenue. From inside a house, mean words were thrown back and forth.

Don't let the dice cool, he thought, or your heart'll grow old.

Down the back streets and alleys, his Army coat hunched up, the black stocking cap pulled down over his ears, he noticed no one; he brooded.

And often it happened that he would stop and smell the air, like that it was burnt or something. Strangers came in low and sideways, talking razor sharp and dreaming in words.

Or say he's walking by some Cazzies now, booting cut over on the sidelines. They was strung out pretty good, spoke in Mau-Mau and tongues. But it grew quiet when he passed.

"Boy is got de humbug," one of them said.

To him it was all inwardness, hell broth, the odor of cordite in the razzmatazz world, and moons blasting down—only when he focused on them, it was the haloes from streetlights dusting the hardware of the town.

He was on the outskirts of Ybor City. He couldn't seem to get in.

It was just Bloods now, and the cars down here got 10-day tags. There was a couple children woke up and stared out a window at the stranger passing. They smiled at each other when he was out of sight—got under the covers!

Heavy guns miles away, and ordnance walking closer down the big-eared dark.

At the corners of side streets, small knots of people watching.

Men within cracked buildings staring in anger and disbelief.

Men of Swahili, men of dreadlocks, and the music of the jungle cutting through these raw surroundings. Down on the backside of town held something sacred about, and he stared at all of this and saw none of it. For he was looking at figures that ran toward him and ran away. Guns played on it, rifles innumerable, a whole stream of tracers, the world in motion and he at the center of it astonished.

Then suddenly he came back into his body. He'd picked up footsteps behind him, caught a blade flash in the corner of his eye once when he turned.

Can you fucking believe it? he said to his mind. Night Train, Mombo, what shall I call thee? And there at a streetlight he sent his shadow on alone, though it hesitated to go in front.

The knife bit him once on the forearm like a little animal. He hit the blade and it flew away. He held him there at arm's length—was it a man? He looked it square in the face. Nothing. No machinery in the eyes.

He marked his place. They're at the start of a bridge, railroad tracks down below, different colors of broken glass along the spur flashing like a bracelet.

"Why?" this joker says. He kind of squeaked it. It's all he gets out before the left came whistling, and the man went over the railing backwards. A sound like a rat screaming. Then afterwards it's quiet, as if nothing happened in the first place.

Shit, he thought. Man … I didn't thought I'd dropped him that hard. He just looked around then. He wanted to ask somebody if they had any wraps. He just felt like, like he might want a burn one now. He looked around to ask somebody if they had any wraps, but he was on the bridge alone.

Why? he asks me. Why, motherfucker … because I like it! But he didn't look down. He didn't want to know anymore. He would leave it at that. A page of newspaper scraped along the concrete. That's it, he thought. Yeah. That's good. I jus' won't read the papers for a couple, three days. He laughed dementedly into his hands. Man says *Why*. Then he danced wildly on the bridge and got to howling real pretty like how he would do.

And when he crossed the bridge, he spoke the commandments to himself one by one:

(The First Commandment) *It is time to move with absolute and correct violence.*

And he answered aloud: "Pray for me."

(The Second Commandment) *Kill coldly and you will be saved.*

A black car hurtled by, its gas to the floorboard. Who was driving is anyone's guess. Below the streetlight colors skated off the chrome. And he answered to himself: "Pray for me."

Heavy guns miles away, and nowhere to turn—all the back doors guarded by big boys with pinheads. I've ruined my hands on them, he thought, ruint them on bald heads. His mind screamed this, yet his voice floated dumb in his mouth.

Those who saw him pass now grew suspicious of this divine being who stalked the night, his expression almost childish, but his eyes separated him from his looks. It would take four sleeps to forget him.

They noted that he would make a small, deranged laugh and shake his head as if to clear it, and this would repair his face to the oddness of before.

Heavy guns miles away, and the earth shuddered underfoot.

His body was walking to the right of him and seemed preoccupied with staring at the sidewalk. Then he would get hold of himself momentarily and resume in the flow of the town, in that strange hour now when the people the night had cast aside would pass those going to work.

He stopped just then—and howled! Now his voice and mind were one, and it scratched the air coming forth.

Two old reptiles of the evening *cocked they head.* People at the bus stop turned to each other, even to those they didn't know and said, "What the hell was that?" Sailors felt their back pockets. Three whores stopped to look at him, and one was heard to comment, "This is turned into one them evenings what has wandered off the path."

But one of these recognized a despair she had often felt herself, for she was the littlest whore in Tampa. And drawn by his voice, by the magnitude and the wilderness in it, she confronted him and yanked him out of a story from the Bible, Revelations perhaps, in which he had been sorely lost. And maybe he thought he was talking to an angel, it's not clear, or to a leprechaun say, but he spoke as follows:

"I don't know if you'll understand. I been beaten up by fighters that was miles away. Devils roared overhead, and shellfire rattled the world till nothin' left was solid. All was hell broth, and I was sneakin' around the alleys a this, tryin' to get in the back way...."

"Lis'en t'you. Jus' lis'en you," the littlest whore in Tampa said. "Shit ... you 'as jus' alone, an' a man alone is in bad company."

# 29. ADDING IT UP

Friday night, Wade got a call at the bar. Sparky held her hand over the phone. "Wade," she said, "it's for you. I think it's that friend a yours." Sometimes Sparky remembered Kuka's name, and sometimes she didn't.

"Tell him to wait five minutes, then call the 7-Eleven number. He'll know what I'm sayin'."

Down at the corner store five minutes later, the pay phone rang. Wade picked it up.

"Is Angel there?" a man's voice asked.

"You got the wrong number."

"Who the hell are you?" it said.

Wade slammed the phone down. "Asshole," he said. Then it rang again.

"Hey."

"This you?"

"Yeah. What's up? You in town?"

"No," Kuka said. "Say ... I ran into some information. I don't know what it's worth, but you need to hear it. It comes through Hazel from Madonna."

"This ought a be good," Wade said.

"Madonna says Mick's in with the cops."

Wade was silent for awhile. "Damn," he said. He thought some more. "Might not be so crazy as it sounds. Somebody broke in the car after you left. Stole them 'ludes I had. Took my Army jacket. Mick'd been around. He's the only one knowed I had that shit there. So he either took it, or he had help. Told 'em where to look, say. Why the fuck they took my jacket I got no idea. It pissed me off. I could a give a shit about the dope."

"Maybe they was cold," Kuka offered.

Wade held the phone away from his face a moment, looked at it quizzically.

"Whatever," he said. "But I'm thinkin'—it's got a be Mickey. Ain't no way 'round that. It's the only way it adds up, right?"

"Yeah," Kuka said, an' somethin' else. I was thinkin' the other day 'bout when you brought his girlfriend around...."

"What you talkin' about?"

"I'm talkin' 'bout Johnnie, goddamn it."

"When was I to 've done that?"

"I'm thinkin' on to way back, when we was at the other place. An' must've been at Emma Street, too."

"How'd you know 'bout that?"

"She tole me … in a round about way. Says to me one night at the bar, 'You got a nice place there.' Some shit. It took me awhile to figure it, you know. 1 an' 1 is three, an' so forth. An' Mick said somethin' to me once. We both so fucked up at the time, it didn't make sense. But anyway … so, there you go."

"Shit," Wade said.

"I thought it was her sister you was foolin' with."

"I remember it else wise."

"How you mean?"

"Well," Wade said, "it was both. Both of 'em. Sometimes both at once …."

Kuka said, "Oh boy. Well, here's another thing. Cecil's been hangin' 'round with Madonna."

"You're kidding."

Wade thought awhile on that. Then he said, "Okay … that's good. That's good. It means I can find his ass now." He was quiet some then. "Fucking Mickey … he ain't the same as he used to was … I knew that…."

"You seen him?"

"Not since I got broke into. This is weeks ago…. After you left town. He's dropped out a sight. Nothin'. But I know he's around, see. I know that."

"Damn," Kuka said. After awhile he said, "How's Keli?"

"She's okay now."

"What you mean, now?"

"It's a long story … I fucked a midget. Got the clap. So now she's got it. A long story, like I say. But look, I got a chance to go to Paris. Keli can get a job there as an exchange student. Paris, France I'm sayin'. So I'm thinkin' 'bout goin' over there with her for a year. I got to work some things out first. But I'm thinkin' on it. How 'bout you, want a come along, too?"

"I don't know," Kuka said. "It means I'd have to fly, right?"

"Yeah, that's what it means I suspect. Lest you want a take a fucking boat."

"When's this gonna happen?"

"Right after Christmas."

"That ain't very far away."

Wade said, "Think it over. How's it goin' with you anyways?"

"Not bad."

"How's this place yer stayin'?"

"It's okay. It looks like an old chicken farm. But O'Neil's raising fighting cocks. That's close as it gets to bein' legit. But it's all right. It's on a lake. There ain't neighbors to speak of. The icebox's full a fish, rabbit, quail, all kinds a shit. O'Neil made *beaucoup* on his reef—

that what he growed this year. Five grand ...."

"Damn!"

"Him an' the old lady's up to Alabama till after the new year. I'm jus' lookin' after the place. I feed his dogs. He left me some smoke— it's good, I'll say that. But it gets a little boring here. I don't hardly see nobody. You get to thinkin' 'bout givin' the broom a trim sometimes."

Wade said, "I'm gone need a place to stay after Christmas—jus' for a day or two."

"You got it."

"Call me in a week, ten days. I'll know more about this Paris thing by then. Let's see. What else? That little drawler a yers is been around. She's stickin' pretty close to Keli. I don't know if she's waitin' for you to show up or what."

"Nell Jordan?" Kuka said.

"Yeah. Look—I got a get back."

"I'll see you after Christmas, then."

Wade said, "You hear 'bout Deuce?" But Kuka'd already hung up.

# 30. THE DOOR PRIZE

Wade bought a car. There was a regular at the bar named Bennie. Down the street a block or so, he owned a used car lot. It didn't have no name. It just said in big letters: BUY HERE PAY HERE. This is what he did legitimately. What he did otherwise was to make book. He ran a little card parlor; you could put down a couple bob on an NFL game there, things of this nature. So Bennie sold it to him, 25 a week, and if Wade got tired of it, he was to bring it back.

Bennie interrupted a game to point out his stock. He pointed out several that were solid. He had a cigar stub in one corner of his mouth, which he removed now, as if for clarity of speech.

Then he threw it down. He took a new cigar from his shirt pocket. He showed it to Wade, and then admired it himself.

He said: "Hoyo de Monterrey. Excaliber Numero Uno. Claro wrapper. Good...."

Wade looked at it. The cigar was about eight inches long.

"Good Tampa cigar," Bennie said.

Then he pointed to some of his cars. Wade decided on a Buick. It was one of them sleds everybody ditched about then. It was jet black and had balloon whitewalls.

Bennie sat back down at the table and looked at his hand. He was playing some of his associates—Odious Barfield, Johnnie Skow, Buster O'Lone. They were playing 7-card stud. They all knew Wade. If they wasn't there at the card table, they was at the bar. Bennie handed over the keys.

"It's an attractive item," he remarked. But the boys, they was pretty much bemused at the fact a white man had bought it.

Wade went looking for Mickey. He looked for Cecil. Mickey had disappeared altogether. Soon word got around that Mick was in jail. Everyone could accept this. Then they said he was in prison up at Jackson, Michigan. This made no sense at all, but it was passed on anyway.

When Wade got off work, he'd have breakfast down near Hyde Park. Afterwards he'd drive by Madonna Smith's. Or sometimes he wouldn't eat, just park down the street from her house. One night a light was on, and a knock came to her door. When she saw who it was, a kind of sick feeling took her, like say you run into someone you still got it bad for.

"It's late."

"I ain't sleepy," he said.

Her gown was made of fine linen, it was want to fall off her shoulder, she wore a gold chain on her ankle, and that was all he noticed really other than her beauty. She was pretty. There wasn't no two ways about that.

"I been thinkin' 'bout you," she said.

"Sure," Wade said.

They sat down in the living room. They sat there for awhile, one on each side of the couch, not talking. There was about them the sadness of people waiting at a bus stop. That strange expression of not really looking at anything.

It's funny how it goes, he thought. This room once held promise. But things weren't so nice anymore. The air was stale. He strained to recall what had brought him to this place to begin with, back at the start of it all. Then Madonna opened her legs like a fan and closed them, and he remembered.

She had a bottle of Benedictine on the end-table. She poured herself a glass, stared into the drink.

There'd been two, three worlds between them, and now he was in reach. Just to be hooked on his arm again, walking down the street in the evening. Then she started thinking about his rig, and the room got in dangerous close and made itself known.

Pretty soon she spoke:

"I talk to my girlfriends. Say to them about you an' me, how we used to do this together an' that ... an' I keep wonderin' what went wrong?"

She was looking at him, but he was concentrating somewhat off to one side. Then he turned his face, looked through her as if she had no reality whatsoever.

She started to get angry. It was just one of his moves, and she'd seen them.

"That kind a shit is somethin' I been wantin' to talk on," she said. But she stopped, got on keel. The temper was in her like dirty fire, and she let it go out.

"I've missed you," she said. "I ain't over it. You ruint me on other men." She said it like that.

"No one can match up. Jus' boys get drunk an' go stupid on me."

"You want I should put on my boots or lift my feet?" he said.

She opened her mouth once again but didn't say nothing. She tried it again. "Wade, I'm doin' my level best not to get mad." Then she started over.

"When you didn't come home that night, it was jus' like some kind a shakedown. Like that I had taken all my feelin's an' showed 'em to a cop or somethin'. 'Cause I thought ... that we had something, what you always dream about. An' I'd be puttin' on corn to boil, an' I'd think about you, or fryin' bacon in the morning ... I'd turn to yell somethin' to you in the bedroom ... an' I'd remember. An' the only thing worse than wonderin' what yer old man's fuckin' ... is knowin'.

"Connie's sister let me have it all. What's that bitch's name?" And she laughed kind of and shook her head. "I guess I'm jus' too fragile for this rough trade. I was, when I ... to think someone loves you ... then find out different like that. I like to never got that through my head. It was like that I'd been livin' with a spy. Like you weren't you no more. You were them ... an' they're murder."

Wade stood up. He stuffed his hands in his pockets.

"Cecil," he said. "Talk says you an' him, that you hangin' around together. That true?"

"Yeah," she said. "Some."

"Where can I find him?"

"How should I know? Besides, listen, he ain't the one put the touch on you."

"That don't matter no more."

"What is it with you?" she said. "This thing with Cecil ... it's jus' like with me, ain't it? You make shit up in yer mind, an' keep everyone on edge with it. An' you love it—to make everyone like you, what don't trust nothin' ... you're sick. A sick motherfucker." They were angry words, but she said them calmly.

"That ain't what matters," Wade repeated.

Madonna sort of smiled then, but there wasn't anything in it—like someone will do when they ain't been listening. But she smiled and moved her head in a way that was peculiar to her and moved her body just a little, and he started smelling her.

So he smelled her, and she seemed to transform someway, how a woman will who is in must. On that same level, she noticed the change had occurred everywhere, and she moved her body again. And her gown looked like trouble was going to break out in several places all at once. His rig started dealing with this on its own, and she understood, and her feelings were getting all kinds of out of hand. But he was the same and was torn between this and his purpose.

"Cecil," he said, but she wasn't listening to any of that.

She laid on her belly on the couch and displayed them secrets of hers. They were considerable. Now Wade reached down and juggled his balls a couple times, said, "Girl, yer fixin' to run me hot."

Madonna spread her legs apart some and whispered, "Lamb's bread...."

Then a thing or two happened that sometimes will. It didn't last but less than nowhile.

A she-wolf fed and whimpered. A horse screamed.

It was decadent, harsh, sublime. "It was ever'thing," Madonna would tell her girlfriend, Mary Redhead, the next day over the telephone.

When he took it away from her, she lay there not turning to face him.

"Cecil's down in Ybor. There's an apartment over the old glass store ... look," she said. "Maybe you could stay. I don't mind some trouble...."

He didn't say nothing, said in his thoughts: Baby, what you jus' got was the door prize.

Madonna, departure into the sadness and beauty of a name. Within the month she married a fiddle player from a club down on Swann Avenue, and they moved to L.A. People who knew the musician felt bad for him.

# 31. THE GHOST TRAIN

Wade pulled into the driveway at Emma Street one Saturday evening—it was nearly dark—and a car followed and parked behind him.

It was December 11th. He'd been to the supermarket and bought what he needed to make spaghetti for him and Keli. He liked making spaghetti, and then he liked eating it even better. Also, his mind was running through a fight that'd been on TV at the bar. Bobby Chacon had taken a 15 round decision against Bazooka Limon, the WBC title holder. Several times during the bout, Chacon was out of it. Then he'd come back. These were super featherweights, but they both carried a big punch. Limon, a southpaw, swung awkward, looping lefts he kept tagging Chacon with. At one point the referee grabbed Bobby Chacon's gloves. He was saying something to him—Can you go on? Chacon's eyes were dead, but you could see even on the television, what he told the referee was, "Fuck you." And he'd come back into the fray again. Then it'd turned into something different. Just heart and balls out there. In the 13th round, Chacon upped the ante. He had the champion wobbly, but Limon was saved by the bell. With fifteen seconds left in the bout, Chacon knocked him down with one of his right hand leads, and took the title.

So Wade had spaghetti and Bobby Chacon on his mind, and all a sudden there's a car behind him. He looked in the rearview mirror. It was Mickey's sister. He understood this as a sign that he was losing touch with his world.

He walked back to the car and said, "Hey, Anita."

"Wade," she said, "Mickey's gettin' out...." She expressed this excitedly, out of breath, somewhat overcome with joy at the prospect of it, say. Wade thought, I guess now he'll know where I live.

She was much older than Mick, a plump woman with hair above her mouth, who blinked excessively. Mickey had mentioned to the boys in passing once that if she put a watch on her wrist, time would stop. He was serious. From then on, they viewed her with some awe. But in truth, she was otherwise so frighteningly ordinary it was impossible to match her with her brother. She could pass for his mother or aunt, perhaps, and she treated Mickey as one of these might, blind to what he was all about.

"Gettin' out a where?" Wade asked.

"He's been to Jacksonville for drug rehab."

He was going to say something, but it never went anywhere.

"I have to get on," she said. "I was jus' out to do some shoppin', an' I saw you. I thought you'd want a know."

"Thanks, Anita," he said.

He walked down to the paper machine, got a *Tribune* and began looking through the classifieds for another place to live.

That next evening, Mickey called him at work.

"Hey," Mick says, "I'm gettin' out in a couple, three days. There any good shit around?"

"Where you callin' from?"

"Six-Mile Creek."

"You think I gone stupid or what?" He dropped the phone, left it dangling. He just couldn't believe it. For Mickey to call him from jail and ask something like that.

Wednesday night, Mickey came to the bar. He didn't go inside, that was out of the question. But he haunted the parking lot. Pretty soon Wade heard that he was out there. He stayed in, killing the sadness, not being cautious, not fearful—that wasn't his way—just lost momentarily in the blood of the rituals of a gone time.

Then he went outside. At the house behind the bar, he saw Venetian blinds being drawn to block out the Tampa night—briefly a hand on the cord like blown glass.

Mick stood near the street, his shadow on the ground, cast down long and thin by the streetlight.

Those who'd seen him already told Wade they had spoken to Mick, but there was no recognition as such. They'd noted how terribly fucked up he was. And Wade thought, Yeah, the cops give him some real good shit to take with.

Mickey there near the street, his body twitching in smoky Dilauded night, leaning against the darkness, now against the light, snoring on his feet.

Wade spoke inwardly: Go on, Mick. It ain't you no more anyways. Don't leave yer death here ... not on my hands.

Mick leaned too far and nodded awake in the midst of stumbling, caught himself, then put his hands on his knees and threw up.

And he rose too fast from this and fell over backwards in a slow dream-like way and sprawled on the pavement unconscious.

Wade picked him up and carried him to Keli's car. There was a T-shirt in the car, and he tried to clean Mickey up some. Set him over in the shotgun seat and drove down toward the river. He took him to the old deserted house by the river that everyone called The Ghost Train. He carried him into a long room dominated by a stone fireplace and a staircase with a wide landing and a window seat. The floor was dark red tile. The house had been beautiful once, but now it was all trashed, and he laid Mickey down in the wasted room among the broken window glass and rubble and owl shit.

Mickey was breathing ugly. Wade took off his flannel shirt and

put it over him, said:
"You went too far this time."
He tucked the shirt around him.
"There ... a man like you," he said, "is got a look his best."

Somewhere toward dawn of the next morning, Kuka dreamed:
*He and Mickey and Wade sat cross-legged in a room without furniture. The walls and ceiling were like that of a Quonset hut. A lantern flickered and made them all look strangely primitive. Mickey leaned against the far wall with his head thrown to one side, like that he was sleeping.*

*Kuka turned and regarded Wade. He wore, Kuka felt, the same heavy and emotionless expression that he himself did. They seemed to be waiting in this room, but no one said why.*

*He noted that Mickey had on white shoes, white pants, a powder-blue shirt, a white coat and tie, and that a Panama hat rested at his side. He looked like a sideshow rendition of a Southern planter. He was all in white linen, his shirt was lightly starched. But it was like that someone had dressed up a wino. In the dream this did not seem out of place. Kuka took it in but did not question anything.*

*Well all of a sudden this young angel appeared amongst them. She was lovely. The light did some games with her face. She wore the silk tunic and trousers of the ao dai. She had big, grave eyes. But you did not notice this so much, for her actions were like a child lost in play.*

*"I hate to sing my own praises," she began. Her voice was thick with drugs, but Kuka thought, She talks like someone from another country.*

*Her clothes made a strange echo when she moved. She seemed to do some things out of focus.*

*He looked more closely. She was naked. She was hanging from a rope. Kuka realized he had seen this act once before at a cheap carnival. But the woman in that instance had been almost unbelievably fat. This was much different, and his eyes could not turn away. They became no more than cameras rolling on a scene so absurd and sensuous that his whole body began to stutter in orgasmic excitement.*

*Then Wade picked up on something that wasn't right. He tried to tell Kuka, but the light changed just then from rawest yellow to deep blue. This confused his words for a moment, but finally he got it across.*

*"She's chewin' betel nut," he said.*

*Kuka did a double-take and saw that her smile was black, but he couldn't place what that meant.*

*"Nickel, dime or a quarter," she was saying to Mickey, "an' if you don't get it now, it's your own damn fault ...." And there was Mick, his head thrown to one side.*

Kuka spoke into the dream. He said it eloquently, but when he sat bolt upright in the bed awake, he was just mumbling something incomprehensible.

In real life, Mickey didn't die. He came back from that night—but he didn't come all the way back.

You might see him still down in Sulphur Springs. He rides an old bicycle around there. Sometimes, if the Sulphur Springs pool is open in the summer, he'll be there outside the fence, leaning on it, looking at the young girls, his face all puzzled. Don't look directly into his eyes.

# 32. AMMO

Wade went to see Billy Lyle. Billy was tall, lanky, his body all angles. He'd been a demolitions man, one of the best along the DMZ. Shrapnel from a 122 rocket got a part of his right leg, March 5, 1968, Camp Carroll. So now he wore a brace. The leg was bowed unnaturally, and constituted the only curve on his whole frame.

His talk was crazy most the time. There was a confinement of purpose to it. He was one of those might be in the newspapers some day. But if you was from over there, sometimes what he had to say did not seem that outrageous. Or say you're somebody else—if you stayed off that straight line between where he was coming from and where he was going, he wouldn't fuck with you. He had the sort of attitude Wade thought much of. A straight, simple man—I smell it, I see it, I waste it.

Billy's wife, Jobeth, was sitting in the living room with their son, Brock. Brock was two then. She'd been reading to him out of a storybook called *The Bear and the Peanut Butter Jar*. They were sharing a can of Chek soda. Wade asked if it'd be all right if him and Billy talked private. She replied:

"Surely. Are you hungry, Wade? There's some city chicken in the icebox. It's good."

"No thank you, ma'am ," he said.

"Well," she said, "it's nice to see you again."

"Thank you, ma'am," Wade said. "The feelin's likewise."

Jobeth was a Christian woman. She was just plain and good. What her and Billy had together never made too much sense to Wade. She loved him truly, and he tolerated that about her. And secondly, she believed devoutly in Christ, and Billy had that kind of deep faith, also, though his was to plastics. So he wore the pants in the family, and she was the heart, and they respected this other thing that each thought much of, though neither had any interest or feeling for it.

"C'mon into the study," Billy said.

He said, "We've been had some trouble with the neighbors. There's Guineas over to the left of us. A young couple. Nice folks, far as I can see. But Jobeth, she's hard-shell Baptist, you know. She'd like to make hell spic & span if she could. An' she jus' about can't stand a Catholic. It don't matter that you're one. That's different somehow.

"That other side we got a bunch a heathens. They like to knock the shit out each other. I tell ya, Wade, this fucking neighborhood, you got a bad muffler an' you talk loud. That's about the size of it. The weekends are accompanied by gunfire and the consumption of bottled goods...."

Well as he was saying this, a disturbance commenced to make itself heard.

"Hit me, motherfucker. Do it. Gone ... it'll make you feel like a man...." This kind of thing.

"That's what I mean," Billy said.

They lived on a little side street up by Busch Gardens. You could see the top of a huge ride at the end of the block.

"I'm gonna put Brock to bed," Jobeth yelled out. "He don't need to be hearin' that."

"Gone. Jus' fuckin' do it. Fire one off...." And it went on like that.

"C'mon chickenshit! Right here ... go ahead, plant one. Yer such a big fucking deal."

Well pretty soon there was the sound of a blow being struck.

Wade and Billy looked out the window. The chick had her face plastered to the driveway. He'd put her down cold.

All of a sudden, Jobeth opened the kitchen door and hollered, "What's goin' on out there?"

The chick in the driveway lifted her head, trying it out, then focused somewhat toward the house and screamed at it:

"MIND YER OWN FUCKIN' BIDNESS!"

They sat down.

"How you been, Wade?"

"All right," he said. "But you know how it goes. Everything's subject to change 'cept the bullshit."

"You still seein' that Smith girl?"

"That was a while back," Wade said.

"She's a pretty thing," Billy said. "I think I had 'bout half a crush on her myself."

"That was some time ago," Wade said. "She needs a boy what's already docked. An' to get rid a little of herself. Accordin' to her, you know, she walks on water ... but it's made out a ice."

Billy nodded, thought to himself, *I see*. He said aloud, "What's Kuka up to?"

Wade smiled some.

"Hard to say. You never know about that boy."

It was an extra bedroom Billy had made into his study. Rifles and shotguns took up the walls, pistols in holsters and knives all about, ammo boxes stacked one on the other, cartridge belts. He had his dress uniform in the closet. He had this and that. He even had a crossbow.

"What's on yer mind, son?" Billy said.

"I need somethin'. I don't know if you got any."

"Name it."

"I need a couple grenades."

Billy's face lit up.

"Yer talkin' more'n a hot foot, then?"

"Yeah," Wade said.

"What you got in mind," Billy said, "an' let me see if I got this straight now, yer talkin' shitstorm ... somethin' long that line?"

"That's about it."

"Well, look," Billy said. "I got some C4, now ... *beaucoup* ... got caps for it."

"Grenades be all right. Nothin' fancy. I can pull a pin."

"This is great! This is fucking great!" Billy had started rummaging through some drawers. He couldn't find nothing for awhile. "It's the way it'll be some motherfucker breaks in here ... I won't be able to find shit. Here we go. All right ... I got yer standard asskicker here." Come to find out he had more than a few.

"I jus' need a couple," Wade said.

"Jus' two?" Billy shook his head and grinned. "He jus' need two."

"What I owe you?"

"I'll put it on the cuff," Billy said. "Better yet, how 'bout I help out?"

"It's somethin' I got a do alone."

"Damn it t'hell, Wade ... I don't never get to have no fun." He picked up a twelve-gauge sawed-off pump, racked a load. "I should a stayed there, goddamn bad wheel an' all." He looked at the door, listened at it. When he talked again, he kept his voice low. "Had all the pussy a man could take ... had money I didn't know what to do with. Tomorrow, say ... if I was there, I'd go fuck with some them little yella bastids. You know, jus' for entertainment.

"This bullshit here ... ain't what it's cracked up to be. Like pullin' some kind a sentence, an' you ain't even in jail."

He took his uniform coat off the hanger and tried it on, and it fit perfectly.

"Who is the asshole in question here, Wade?" Billy said. "He ain't a vet is he?"

"No," Wade said. "It's Cecil."

"Oh, well ... there you go. I know who you mean—that dude looks like a damn camel in the face ... I've seen him at the bar. Fuck him. Wade," he said looking at himself in the mirror, "you ain't seen a thing, lest you experience one of my set-ups...."

Wade thought about that for some time.

"Billy," he said then, "let's talk...."

## 33. FLOWER-SCATTERING-CHILD

Billy said over the phone, "He's here. Give me a half-hour, forty minutes. I'll meet you in the alley."

"How's it been down there?"

"Early on there was a fight. Wadn't no punches thrown, jus' a lot a fussin'. Last couple hours it's jus' me an' two studs with purses."

Someone came up to the phone then and asked Billy a question.

"What?" Billy said.

"Fuck off!" he said. "Hey, I'll say it again so's you can total it up." Then to Wade, "Jesus...."

"What's up?"

"This character what's been lookin' through the dumpster comes over an' asks me can I spare a quarter for a tourist. I'll tell ya, I'm glad this shit's 'bout over. It's lowlife Eldorado down here."

Billy'd been on recon four nights. He talked to some whores the first night he's in Ybor, found out that Cecil drank in a bar called The Alibi. Billy went there and started studying him.

Turns out Cecil's got some habits. He'd come to the bar late, usually after midnight. Whatever time he come in, he'd stay till it closed, play some pool, get shit-faced, then walk home. He had the way home down right, no matter how wrong he was at the time.

The bartender there, who considered himself somewhat an orator, had filled Billy in on Cecil and about everyone else who came in the place. He'd leer around drunk as the rest of them. Every time trouble broke out, he'd yell, "I don't want no conflictions in here!" But no one paid him any mind whatsoever.

The neighborhood abouts was pretty raw. Wasn't a lot of choices say if you lived around there. You was on the dodge, you was on edge, you didn't laugh out loud too much. A lot of these came in the bar, and others involved in the dark dollar, and scattered amongst them were longshoremen who spoke different languages and their dates who wore nice dresses and too much make-up, but sometimes needed a shave, and young boys with their hair butch waxed, and some old Cuban men who drank silently in their Spanish depression—it's possible they had lived long enough to be aware that something was very wrong.

They'd all take a polite serving of bullshit early on, but after they got torched up, arguments would begin. Billy drank too much and acted like an asshole. If you did that, didn't nobody notice you then.

Billy sat at the bar awhile longer. He observed Cecil once more, thinking—After tonight bud, yer career is gonna go into a serious decline.

Cecil was playing pool. He slouched when he stood. His long

head hung forward from his body. His nose was bulbous, and he had big, haunted eyes. The harelip had been fixed badly, and it gave him an odd, broken smile—though he did not smile much, nor did he talk a lot. Whatever he was doing seemed to irritate him. When someone was speaking to him, he'd hold his head sideways and stare fishily at them.

Wade took a cab down to Ybor, as Billy had his car, and they met in the alley behind Cecil's flat. The bottom floor was deserted. It'd been a stained-glass shop at one time. To one side was a laundry and to the other a pawn shop. But it stood empty, and Cecil lived on the second floor. Billy'd already been up there and rigged it.

Wade put his hand on the fire escape. The air smelled of coffee from one of the coffee mills nearby. He put his hand on the fire escape, then took it back.

"Don't worry 'bout no prints," Billy said. "I create a very dense environment."

"Anybody see you?"

"This young whore cut through here. Kind a yella girl. She looked real young. I asks her how much she wants. Twenty bucks. I wasn't really serious. I was jus' playin' around, you understand." Billy smiled. "Then she says out a the blue, I don't eat tongue an' I don't goes on trains."

"Wha'd you say to that?"

"I didn't say nothin'. I didn't know what the fuck she was talkin' about. Then she left. She looked good. Had an ass on her all right, but her teeth wasn't so nice. Kind a missin' one or two."

"What about the place?"

"It's set." He looked up to the sky. "Got a fine night for it. No rain. Good cloud cover ... take care you don't touch nothin' too hard up there."

Wade nodded and climbed the fire escape.

He looked around the room. It was a room with a bed and toilet and a dresser with the veneer curling off. There was a yellow chair and a blue glass on the floor beside it. An overflowing ashtray, numerous packs of cigarettes that were flat and folded in half, an empty pint of Jim Beam. Rising from the midst of this, as if drunk from the surrounding disorder, was a wobbly metal lamp with a paper shade cocked at an angle. That was about it. One side of the building had settled, and everything in the room was crooked.

The neon sign from the pawn shop next door blinked slowly on and off, so that one moment a dark red owned the room, then the next it turned black. Here and there were Billy's set-ups, blasting caps hooked to plastic, and some fancy gear—who knows what that was all about— some of Billy's inventions, and there were detonating wires leading out to the adjoining roofs, what they used to call quarry cord when Wade was a kid. He looked out the window to where Billy had been standing, but didn't see him. He'd already gone to the car, or else it was like how he'd do sometimes, where, lest he moved, you'd forget he was around because he'd be practicing his camouflage.

So Wade just waited, thought. Billy's comment about the cloud cover hadn't meant much to him, and he didn't stay with it long. What most concerned him was the curse. All the past week Billy'd told him about that if a dying man knew his killer's name, he could put a humbug on him. But Wade thought now, That's jus' too bad. He had it in his mind that he wanted Cecil to know exactly how this went down.

Ybor City droned on outside. Now and then a car'd barrel down the avenue, running on that sweet high-test, and sometimes much slower, the voices of winos stumbled into the room. Finally there was a noise on the stairs. Wade positioned himself off to the side of the door. He heard Cecil fucking with the lock. He was mumbling to himself. Then the door opened.

Cecil shocked at the throat—everything's over now. Wade'd just reached out and spoiled him, a storm flash, and no sound but the larynx buckling, held him there at arm's length against the wall and kicked the door shut. He stared Cecil in the eye, nodded to him oddly, as you might butcher a greeting to someone you didn't really care to see, but Cecil just had this look scrawled across his face. The light next door blinked a couple times, and Cecil mixed into the blood of the air, then disappeared into the dark.

*Cecil. Cecil gone to not. Stood inside the doorway of somethin' wrong and couldn't figure it out.* Some rhyme like that was going through Wade's mind, but all his physical strength was concentrated in his right hand. Cecil sank down the wall, his lips blue, and Wade laughing over him.

He cut off Cecil's ears and fingers and put them in a sack. The room was red/dark—red/dark, and Wade wiped his blade on a curtain, laughing low and dementedly like the sound of a Glas Pac far off.

Then he was outside in the car. Billy drove around the block and came half ways back down. He had what looked like buttons attached to the forefinger and thumb of his left hand, and he held them tight together.

"In the old days," Billy said, "this kind of contraption was called a deadman's switch. This is more sophisticated, you understand. Let's make sure we don't have no civilians in the area ... watch closely now, I'm gone throw the fat on the fire." And he opened his hand.

As Billy drove off, the building danced just briefly, then collapsed in a heap of cinder block, timber and red tile roofing. The blast stuttered the car in its tracks. It uprooted palm trees, blew a door half way down the block. Blew out windows of nearby buildings and cracked their walls; the whole of Ybor City was want to rattle.

This all happened in the time it took to knock your ears dumb. It'd blown clothes out of the laundry, and some of them stuck all over the place, maybe like people was standing around looking there in the rubble, but wasn't no people in them.

They passed a convenience store on the way down to 7th Avenue, and the cash register there spewed yards of tape out onto the sidewalk.

Billy pulled into a parking space. Dogs had started howling.

"We gone shag in a minute here, Wade ... but hold tight a bit. I got a little show cooked up ... crackers up on them roofs." He was looking at his watch. "Just about ... now," he said.

Then tracers shot up into the sky and dangled over the city like red ropes.

"I got some mortar racks up there. Fire-in-the-hole!" he said.

Flares started going off, you could hear the thunk of propellant-shooting canisters, and shells began to shriek into the night. They started popping, and the colors of the rainbow umbrellaed out from them into the shape of flowers and stars and willow sprays.

Dogs and sirens were wailing and Billy said, "Guess we better move on 'fore the cheap suits and guns get here." And they drove slowly down the avenue, taking in the scene yet somehow removed from it, as the people of the city came from houses and bars and stuck their heads out of windows, looking wide-eyed at the fireworks display. Wade and Billy glanced at each other, because the people around there were clapping and cheering and honking their horns as they stared at the sky.

"Wade, you ever want a do this again, you need a leg man, I'm game...." Now there was one last big concussion, and Billy said, "Watch this here. I brought it from Nam. It's a shell called 'Flower-Scattering-Child.'"

As it burst, two white boys passed unnoticed as they went lowriding down 7th Avenue in Ybor City in a prehistoric jet black sled with balloon whitewalls.

The next morning, Wade took his sack out to 22d Street where they bury the paupers, past the wrought iron and marble and weathered angels to the cheap part of the cemetery and the unmarked graves of Potter's Field.

He stood by several new grave sites, but they did not seem to have any feeling to them. Then he saw an old, battle-scarred orange cat sitting by a grave, and he knew it had to be the place. He spread them parts of Cecil on the earth. And damned if the cat didn't come over and smell of them and try to cover it up with dirt. It looked at Wade. It's left eye was totally white. Then it ran up a tree and disappeared. It was all done as if by magic.

"Emmett?" Wade said. "Deuce ... you in there? I know this is a long shot." He looked around for awhile. "I'm jus' gone say this...." He didn't see anybody nearby, so he went on. "You was my friend. I'm sorry we don't get to talk no more. I know we had our differences that one time. You remember that argument when everybody said things they didn't mean ... I forget what it was about...."

He felt embarrassed to be doing this. He wasn't saying it right. He made his hands into fists and opened them, and his fingers started up then like ten dumb tongues, as if he were trying to build words in them.

"Anyways ... I give you these. The man finally outsmarted hisself. I paid him back for you. I paid him back in kind. Dead even. I hope these are of some value to you. Maybe they'll bring you luck. I hope you got out of that box already. That yer in some bar for the ghosts. This shit I put on yer grave here, maybe it'll get you a traveler ... or if there's some pretty thing around say, maybe you can sport her one."

## 34. TRASHED

Wade and Keli would be to O'Neil's the night of the 27th. They'd be staying until the 29th, when their flight left for Paris. Christmas came and went. Kuka only saw one person the whole day—Ruth Huckeba. She was the younger sister of O'Neil's wife, Leona. She'd come around maybe once, twice a week. She'd do her wash there, bring Kuka a sandwich sometimes, clean the place up. If the facts be known, Leona was trying to fix her up with Kuka. Ruth herself was for this arrangement. She thought he was cute or whatever, and she was living across the lake with her Mama and didn't have a whole lot else to think about.

On the other side of this, O'Neil, before he'd left for Alabama, had cautioned Kuka:

"You know Leona's sister, Ruth ... you met her before ... got kind of a big ass on her?"

Kuka remembered that part.

"She's a lunatic," O'Neil said. "She'll be want to talk you to death now."

But it turned out she was all right. The only thing Kuka could see against her was in that she either had only one dress—this sort of faded blue house dress—or else she had many that looked just exactly the same. He kept wondering, What's she washin' all the time?

Well she came over Christmas day and brought him a big plate of food. Turkey, mashed potatoes and gravy, oyster dressing, biscuits, cranberry sauce, the works.

"What's this?" he'd asked her.

"Swamp cabbage an' dumplin's. It's from one of Leona's recipes. I made that myself. Mama did all the rest."

Kuka ate around that.

But it was nice of her to do that, and also it gave him an idea. He wanted to get the makings of a holiday meal, so when Wade and Keli came, they could all sit down to a big dinner like a family.

So he called up John the Hat in town. Kuka needed to sell a couple ounces of smoke, and John usually had cash money on hand for such a purchase. Part of the deal was that he would pick up groceries on his way out. Kuka gave him directions to O'Neil's and read off his list.

"Five cases of Busch, too," he said. He hadn't drank any beer of late.

"You mind if I bring Darla with me?"

"Darla McCluskey?"

"Herself. She's down from Gainesville for a couple days."

"Leave her husband there in town."

"He ain't here."

"Oh my," Kuka said. A smile spread through the line.

Now John the Hat and Darla came out there the day after Christmas. The three of them had pal-ed around a few summers back. Neither one of them had ever got to her, much to their dismay. Because you couldn't meet Darla and not fall in love with her. She was cut from a fine mold, a prime example of where some good Scot/Irish breeding could take you. Plus they'd got in on it a little late—just right before she married. She'd cultivated both of them at once, too, and they'd managed to get in each other's way. At the wedding, John the Hat, looking over the guests, commented that he and Kuka and possibly the groom were the only males present who hadn't slept with her. She used to make a regular milk run on the rest of them.

The three of them started in where they'd left off. Only it was a little more playful maybe, more tongue-in-cheek. The boys'd still feel her up every chance they got, but everyone knew nothing serious was to come of it now. That wasn't so crucial as it'd once been, though just being around her—that pretty face and bone yellow hair and her perfume like a musky flower—you'd once more begin to feel the weight of it.

The conversations were in this vein:

"I'd sure admire to see them tits again."

"I'd like to help you out, Kuka, but … I don't want Johnny to see 'em. You don't know what it might do to him. Might ruin him."

John the Hat had this clown look to him anyway—he was bald on top, but his hair kind of sprung up around it, like he had a little alley going there—and now he had this big ole crooked grin stretching from about here to there.

"Oh, what the hell," Darla said. And she started to pull her shirt up, but she stopped just short. "No … I jus' can't. My husband made me promise I wouldn't never show 'em to John the Hat." But a second later she let on that she'd do it, only Johnny had to close his eyes.

John did this but very haphazardly.

"That ain't gonna cut it. My husband is seriously pissed off at Johnny," she said to Kuka. "He saw him grab my ass at the weddin'. It was very rude of him to do that, don't you think? 'Specially in public."

"It wasn't he minded that so much," John the Hat commented. "What he got mad at was when you looked around an' saw who'd done it, then made yer tongue do like what it did."

John went to the can then. Soon as he was out of the room, Darla pulled her shirt up around her neck. She put a finger on each nipple—they're a pale peach-rose color—and played with them until they stood up. Then she put her hands to the sides of her tits and pushed them together.

"I like to play with them," she said.

"I know what you mean."

"Kuka, honey.…"

"Yeah."

"Do you have a hard-on?"

"What makes you say that?"

"'Cause I can see it there."

When she heard John coming out of the bathroom, she pulled her shirt back down, and said to him:

"Johnny ... while you was in there, Kuka took out his cock an' showed it to me."

"He didn't?"

"Yes, he did. He's got a tattoo on it. Did you know that?"

"No, I can't say that I did. I ain't looked at Kuka's dick lately."

"Yeah ... it says M O M."

When John went to the kitchen to get another beer, she pulled her shirt up again real quick.

"Johnny, let me ask you somethin' ... do you like to get blow jobs?"

"Sometimes," John said from the kitchen.

"I don't do that very good," she said.

John sat back down on the couch, opened his Busch.

"You might jus' need to practice at it some," he said.

"You think?"

They lit up again. It was O'Neil's purple-stripe. You could only take one toke at a time. They each of them took a drag and commenced to think upon it.

After awhile, out of nowhere, Darla said, "Do you guys ever fuck girls in the ass?"

John the Hat acted somewhat put out.

"I don't believe in that," he said. "I think a girl is got to draw the line somewheres."

Kuka said, "You lyin' sack a shit."

"I don't like it too much," Darla said. "My husband does it to me all the time. He's got this kind a stumpy thang sort a squashed on the top—looks like a doorknob. I jus' close my eyes an' wait till it's over." She appeared to be giving this some earnest thought. "Since we got hitched, he's jus' gettin' weird. He wants me to learn how to blow smoke rings with my pussy. Can you picture that?"

John the Hat was losing it, started saying kind of low but urgently:

"I want some...."

"What Johnny?"

"I want it...."

"What? What's he sayin', Kuka?"

"I want a fuck...."

"What?" She looked at him like she didn't understand the concept, let alone the word.

"Johnny ... is what's it name gettin' hard? His is got a name, Kuka...."

Then at one point she said to Kuka:

"I met your girlfriend at the bar."

"Who?"

"Nell Jordan."

"I don't think I ever known her to go to the bar."

"She was there with Keli Wyatt. I know Keli. We used to go to school together."

"What'd Nell have to say for herself?"

"For you to kiss her ass, I guess. That's what she told me. Tell Kuka to kiss my ass...."

Kuka sat there just kind of burning.

"I believe you still sweet on her," Darla said.

Then he stalked out of the room.

Darla hunched her head down between her shoulders like something loud had just crashed, made a sad little smile, raised her eyebrows and said to John the Hat, "I was only jokin'...."

Then they didn't leave. The three of them partied all the night long. The next morning they kept on. Darla took John the Hat's car into town about 9 o'clock to score some sniff from this guy she knew. After she was gone too long, John the Hat mused:

"I bet she's in there fucking his brains out ... Lord," he said, "that must be jus' like fuckin' a ribbon."

By three in the afternoon, they'd managed to consume every beer in that five cases of it. After the beer ran out, John and Darla left. John the Hat was known for this form of departure. You knew pretty much when he was going to leave by the number of beers left in the icebox. By the time they departed, Kuka was seriously trashed.

Now when Wade and Keli showed up, they knocked on the door, but no one answered. O'Neil's dogs were barking. The door was unlocked, so Wade just walked in. The place looked like a storm had come through and carved it up. Beer cans everywhere, pizza crusts, a big patch of blood on one wall (John the Hat had stumbled into it and bloodied his nose). Kuka was on the kitchen floor. A chair was down beside him, and he sat there where he'd fallen, a plate and some food spilled around and on him. He was weaving a bit.

Wade said to Keli, "There's our boy."

"He's a diamond in the rough, ain't he?" she said.

Kuka was trying to talk to them. He couldn't understand his voice his own self. It sounded like that he was throwing the words down a well.

"What's he doin'?" Keli asked.

Wade said, "Looks to me he's tryin' to butter that napkin."

# 35. MOCKINGBIRD

"You feelin' any better?" Wade said.

"I think I might have a case of the quickstep," Kuka answered.

They were sitting out on the dock. The afternoon had kind of a pumpkin light to it. There was a chop on the lake. They'd been out in the Jon boat earlier, checked the trotline, found nothing, and reset it with cut bait.

Wade was preoccupied. He stared at the water. Things were tugging at him Kuka could see. He hadn't said much all day. He'd brought his barbells with him. He wanted to leave them at O'Neil's. Soon as he unloaded the weights, he'd started lifting. After that he went for a run. Then he swam across the lake and back. He had things on his mind, but as was his way, he wasn't about to let them out. Kuka had seen this all too many times before to worry on it. Plus he himself just pretty much felt like shit.

"When you leavin' tomorrow?" Kuka asked.

"First thing."

"John was tellin' me there was a big explosion down in Ybor City. Had some kind a fireworks display."

"I don't know," Wade said. "I ain't read a paper lately."

From some things said, Wade had added it up that Kuka knew nothing about Deuce, about Mickey, and so on. And he'd decided to leave it at that and not be the one to tell him. John the Hat had made the same decision.

"This is a good place to hide out," Wade said. "Ain't shit around here."

Land O'Lakes then was just a little town that had lost its chances.

"I went down the road. There's a trailer there, looked like some Beaners in it. Otherwise, it's pasture an' grove. Anybody come around?"

"You ever meet O'Neil's wife?"

"I don't think so."

"Her sister comes by sometimes. Her name's Ruth. There's a washing machine in that little shed ... see, that one with the horseshoe over the door? She comes over and washes her clothes. Her an' her Mama's. They got a worm farm across the lake."

"What's she look like?"

"She's got red hair. Kind a buck-toothed."

"I saw her. Got a big ole ass on her?"

"That's her. She's all right. She'll talk yer ear off. Her husband was from Nam. Phu Bai, I think, down where you was. He got killed in that grove over there." Kuka pointed across the lake. "A tractor turned over on him. I pretty much know her life story. Out here, you don't see nobody. You get a little squirrelly. Her and her sister, they both like to cook weird shit. Possum with persimmons and turnip kraut. That sort a thing. I don't know ... I jus' don't know about eatin' a damn possum.

"She brings me egg salad sandwiches. Sometimes she don't get all the shell out. The other day she brought over some corn-cob jelly. 'Fore that was rose-petal jelly. Something she called peach leather. Now that was good. She comes over in her boat. I invited her for dinner tonight. She wants to help Keli with the cookin'."

"Sounds like she'd jus' about bend over backwards for you," Wade said.

"She might a already," Kuka said. "One night she brought over some cherry bounce. It's some kind a drink made from wild cherries. It's strong. She'd already been at it 'fore she got here. I don't know. I might have fucked her that night."

"But you don't recall it exactly?"

"No, I don't. The details are sketchy." Kuka laughed. "She brought two Mason jars of it. I seem to remember her smoking cock. But I ain't at all clear on it. The next time she comes over, she's dressed to kill. Looked like she was goin' to the '57 prom. All she lacked was a corsage. She was hard pressed to look like a schoolgirl, though. But anyways, so I figured something happened that night she brought the cherry bounce. Now she wants me to take her bowling."

The wind picked up from the south then and ruffled the lake surface.

"You see how the water's calm there in that inlet. Where it's protected by that big line a melaneca trees? O'Neil calls that quiet place a wind blossom."

During the hour or so they sat there they saw three otters. Two osprey flew over. One of them was completely white.

When they started back to the house, just when they got off the dock where the sidewalk began, something came clattering down from a cypress tree and hit the concrete. Wade bent down, and picked up a clam.

"See that blackbird there?" Kuka said. "They's called a grackle. They're smart. They drop them mussels down on the cement to break 'em open. They'll do the same with a little turtle."

Kuka showed him O'Neil's fighting cocks chained to their barrels, what was left of them, because he'd taken a lot to Alabama, along with the best of his hounds. He showed him O'Neil's pitbulls. O'Neil kept them in pens. He had a pair of them, and three pups that were about grown.

When they went inside, Keli said, "That one dog, that big wide-headed one, got a brindle color to him—he keeps curling his lip every time I walk by him."

"His name's Rooter," Kuka said. "What he's doin' is, he's smilin' at you. He likes the ladies, don't matter what kind you are."

"They're pitbulls aren't they?" she said.

"Pretty much."

"I thought they was supposed to be mean."

"Yeah. They're real bad. You got a watch out they don't lick you to death."

Somewhere in here, Wade got Kuka to one side.

"We gone shake hands tomorrow. We ain't gone say good-bye."

And Kuka saw in the spurs along his eyes that time was moving.

Then Wade started lifting weights again. Loading up the bars, doing endless repetitions. He found some stilts in the garage O'Neil'd used for finishing drywall in the old days when he worked construction. These distracted him for awhile and got him to laughing trying to master them. But that wore off, and afterwards it was like that he was practicing his moods once more. The flash came, the electricity, a dark weather in the eyes. He started talking in his junkie voice, then in that exaggerated speech pattern of an old, punch-drunk fighter. He just went out on point and stayed there.

Kuka helped Keli finish cleaning up the place. He'd told her that Ruth would be over later to help her cook, but she'd started in on it herself. They were sitting at the kitchen table working on some snap beans.

"Kuka," she started. "I got a message for you from Nell Jordan."

"I heard she was at the bar," he said.

"She says that she loves you."

"I don't think so."

"Let me say it again … now look me straight in the eye. Nell loves you."

"That's hard to believe. After how I did."

"Kuka … you jus' got a pick up the pace a little now. Here's somethin' else—she says if there's any other girls hangin' 'round, like this Ruth for instance, she says they ain't nothin' but squatters."

Kuka smiled.

"She said that?"

"Yeah. Now here's something else again. She's up to North Carolina right now. She's had a piece of the land cleared, and she's bought a little trailer. She's gettin' that set up. Her brother's up there helpin' her."

"She gone live up there?"

"Yes, she is. An' she wants you to come live with her. Would that be all right with you?"

Kuka thought for a moment and said, "Well, I guess it would."

Keli said to herself, That wasn't so hard. Wade had told her the night before, "Jus' have her to come down here, pack his gear, an' tell him it's time to go."

"Okay," Keli said. "Now ... I've got a number I have to call at 3 o'clock this afternoon. What she wants to do is come get you. When's O'Neil comin' back?"

"On the 1st."

"Well, she wants to come get you then. Either then or the next day or whenever she can. I've got to get it all set up today. Now you're sure?"

They didn't eat until quite late. They set up the picnic table out by the lake, directly under the full moon. The moonlight was strong, just coming down like starch. Ruth'd come, and she and Keli got on like old friends. Kuka let Rooter out of his pen. He went directly to where Keli was sitting, lay there on the ground glancing up at her from time to time and smiling like a fool.

"Tonight's blue moon," Keli said. "There won't be another for two, three years."

Kuka looked at the moon, but he thought it did not appear to be blue at all.

Then they began their feast. And whether it was the food or the company or just the realization dawning that he was indeed going to get out of town, Wade came off his mood.

Ruth had brought over two jars of blackberry brandy, and her and Keli commenced to get seriously drunk. Then Keli talked her into smoking some reef, and that turned out to be somewhat of a disaster. Ruth took a couple healthy tokes, sat silently for a moment or so to make sure she wasn't going to overdose and die on the spot. Then she started talking.

"I ain't had this much fun since the time I went to the Oasis Bar," she said. This unfortunately, however, sparked a memory. "Yeah. I was with Doyle, my husband," she said. "Can you picture it? He's over in Viet Nam for two tours, then subsequently gets kilt by a tractor. Two years with Charlie over there in hell, an' he comes home an' dies not a quarter mile from his own house. Am I trippin' or what?" Then for some reason she laughed hysterically for a full minute.

"A fucking tractor!" she all but screamed. "You know they say He only calls them what's ready. But Doyle, he didn't seem ready to me."

Keli said, "This dog won't eat turkey. What's the matter with him?"

She'd thrown down a piece of turkey to Rooter, and he was setting there looking as if he were somehow ashamed that it'd happened.

"You gotta avert yer eyes," Kuka said. "He don't like nobody to watch him eat. I don't know what it's all about."

It was a bright, cool night and the lake was black and gold.

Ruth hit the blackberry brandy again. She started to wobble some then. Suddenly her demeanor turned crucial. "I'm not an alcoholic, I'll tell you that right now," she said, even though she hadn't been asked.

"Doyle was. He was a damn drunk." And everybody kind of went, O Lord, she's back on that.

"It jus' struck me real hard how bad I ain't got over that shit. Now you all," she said, "you boys seem to have it together...."

Kuka and Wade turned their heads on that one. Kuka just blew air out, kind of under his breath.

She went on: "Some a you are jus' old and wise and spoiled."

"Yeah," Wade said. "How come we're still so fucked up then?"

"Goddamn you, Doyle!" She seemed to address this to no one and everyone all at once. Then she hit the brandy till it was gone, looked down into the bottom of the jar. "I knew that man like I know my own pocket. Jus' a damn shame ... a bad piece of luck."

Wade said, "That's what it all is, ain't it?"

But Ruth didn't hear. "I ain't drunk!" she shouted. "See ... I'll take the test...." And she put a finger to the tip of her nose and fell right on over backwards and lay out cold on the ground.

And that's how it ended somehow. Though that night, a mockingbird sang till dawn in the side yard outside Kuka's window—sang deliriously, sang the blues, and imitated a train, took both sides in a bird argument, recalled the plaintiveness of the osprey, the ghostly sadness of the dove, sang like a drunk on Saturday night. In its song, the story got so tangled up, it's hard to say what happened next. But it wasn't nearly so fast, or so interesting afterwards.